# *Stories By English Authors In Germany*

# Stories By English Authors In Germany

Various Authors


PO Box 2211
Fairfield, IA 52556
www.1stworldlibrary.org
First Edition

LCCN: 2003195155

Softcover ISBN: 1-59540-529-1
Hardcover ISBN: 1-4218-0879-X
eBook ISBN: 1-59540-579-8

***Stories By English Authors In Germany***

*contributed by the Charles Family*

*in support of*

*1st World Library Literary Society*

## CONTENTS

## THE BIRD ON ITS JOURNEY

It was about four in the afternoon when a young girl came into the salon of the little hotel at C -- in Switzerland, and drew her chair up to the fire.

"You are soaked through," said an elderly lady, who was herself trying to get roasted. "You ought to lose no time in changing your clothes."

"I have not anything to change," said the young girl, laughing. "Oh, I shall soon be dry!"

"Have you lost all your luggage?" asked the lady, sympathetically.

"No," said the young girl; "I had none to lose." And she smiled a little mischievously, as though she knew by instinct that her companion's sympathy would at once degenerate into suspicion!

"I don't mean to say that I have not a knapsack," she added, considerately. "I have walked a long distance - in fact, from Z -- ."

"And where did you leave your companions?" asked the lady, with a touch of forgiveness in her voice.

"I am without companions, just as I am without luggage," laughed the girl.

And then she opened the piano, and struck a few notes. There was something caressing in the way in which she touched the keys; whoever she was, she knew how to make sweet music; sad music, too, full of that undefinable longing, like the holding out of one's arms to one's friends in the hopeless distance.

The lady bending over the fire looked up at the little girl, and forgot that she had brought neither friends nor luggage with her. She hesitated for one moment, and then she took the childish face between her hands and kissed it.

"Thank you, dear, for your music," she said, gently.

"The piano is terribly out of tune," said the little girl, suddenly; and she ran out of the room, and came back carrying her knapsack.

"What are you going to do?" asked her companion.

"I am going to tune the piano," the little girl said; and she took a tuning-hammer out of her knapsack, and began her work in real earnest. She evidently knew what she was about, and pegged away at the notes as though her whole life depended upon the result.

The lady by the fire was lost in amazement. Who could she be? Without luggage and without friends, and with a tuning-hammer!

Meanwhile one of the gentlemen had strolled into the salon; but hearing the sound of tuning, and being in secret possession of nerves, he fled, saying, "The tuner, by Jove!"

A few minutes afterward Miss Blake, whose nerves were no secret possession, hastened into the salon, and, in her usual imperious fashion, demanded instant silence.

"I have just done," said the little girl. "The piano was so terribly out of tune, I could not resist the temptation."

Miss Blake, who never listened to what any one said, took it for granted that the little girl was the tuner for whom M. le Proprietaire had promised to send; and having bestowed on her a condescending nod, passed out into the garden, where she told some of the visitors that the piano had been tuned at last, and that the tuner was a young woman of rather eccentric appearance.

"Really, it is quite abominable how women thrust themselves into every profession," she remarked, in her masculine voice. "It is so unfeminine, so unseemly."

There was nothing of the feminine about Miss Blake; her horse-cloth dress, her waistcoat and high collar, and her billycock hat were of the masculine genus; even her nerves could not be called feminine, since we learn from two or three doctors (taken off their guard) that nerves are neither feminine nor masculine, but common.

"I should like to see this tuner," said one of the tennis-players, leaning against a tree.

"Here she comes," said Miss Blake, as the little girl was seen sauntering into the garden.

The men put up their eye-glasses, and saw a little lady with a childish face and soft brown hair, of strictly feminine appearance and bearing. The goat came toward her and began nibbling at her frock. She seemed to understand the manner of goats, and played with him to his heart's content. One of the tennis players, Oswald Everard by name, strolled down to the bank where she was having her frolic.

"Good-afternoon," he said, raising his cap. "I hope the goat is not worrying you. Poor little fellow! this is his last day of play. He is to be killed to-morrow for table d'hote."

"What a shame!" she said. "Fancy to be killed, and then grumbled at!"

"That is precisely what we do here," he said, laughing. "We grumble at everything we eat. And I own to being one of the grumpiest; though the lady in the horse-cloth dress yonder follows close upon my heels."

"She was the lady who was annoyed at me because I tuned the piano," the little girl said. "Still, it had to be done. It was plainly my duty. I seemed to have come for that purpose."

"It has been confoundedly annoying having it out of tune," he said. "I've had to give up singing altogether. But what a strange profession you have chosen! Very unusual, isn't it?"

"Why, surely not," she answered, amused. "It seems to me that every other woman has taken to it. The wonder to me is that any one ever scores a success. Nowadays, however, no one could amass a huge fortune out of it."

"No one, indeed!" replied Oswald Everard, laughing. "What on earth made you take to it?"

"It took to me," she said simply. "It wrapped me round with enthusiasm. I could think of nothing else. I vowed that I would rise to the top of my profession. I worked day and night. But it means incessant toil for years if one wants to make any headway."

"Good gracious! I thought it was merely a matter of a few months," he said, smiling at the little girl.

"A few months!" she repeated, scornfully. "You are speaking the language of an amateur. No; one has to work faithfully year after year; to grasp the possibilities, and pass on to greater possibilities. You imagine what it must feel like to touch the notes, and know that you are keeping the listeners spellbound; that you are taking them into a fairy-land of sound, where petty personality is lost in vague longing and regret."

"I confess I had not thought of it in that way," he said, humbly. "I have only regarded it as a necessary every-day evil; and to be quite honest with you, I fail to see now how it can inspire enthusiasm. I wish I could see," he added, looking up at the engaging little figure before him.

"Never mind," she said, laughing at his distress; "I forgive you. And, after all, you are not the only person who looks upon it as a necessary evil. My poor old guardian abominated it. He made many sacrifices to come and listen to me. He knew I liked to see his kind old face, and that the presence of a real friend inspired me with confidence."

"I should not have thought it was nervous work," he said.

"Try it and see," she answered. "But surely you spoke of singing. Are you not nervous when you sing?"

"Sometimes," he replied, rather stiffly. "But that is slightly different." (He was very proud of his singing, and made a great fuss about it.) "Your profession, as I remarked before, is an unavoidable nuisance. When I think what I have suffered from the gentlemen of your profession, I only wonder that I have any brains left. But I am uncourteous."

"No, no," she said; "let me hear about your sufferings."

"Whenever I have specially wanted to be quiet," he said - and then he glanced at her childish little face, and he hesitated. "It seems so rude of me," he added. He was the soul of courtesy, although he was an amateur tenor singer.

"Please tell me," the little girl said, in her winning way.

"Well," he said, gathering himself together, "it is the one subject on which I can be eloquent. Ever since I can remember, I have been worried and tortured by those rascals. I have tried in every way to escape from them, but there is no hope for me. Yes; I believe that all the tuners in the universe are in league against me, and have marked me out for their special prey."

"All the what?" asked the little girl, with a jerk in her voice.

"All the tuners, of course," he replied, rather

snappishly. "I know that we cannot do without them; but good heavens! they have no tact, no consideration, no mercy. Whenever I've wanted to write or read quietly, that fatal knock has come at the door, and I've known by instinct that all chance of peace was over. Whenever I've been giving a luncheon party, the tuner has arrived, with his abominable black bag, and his abominable card which has to be signed at once. On one occasion I was just proposing to a girl in her father's library when the tuner struck up in the drawing-room. I left off suddenly, and fled from the house. But there is no escape from these fiends; I believe they are swarming about in the air like so many bacteria. And how, in the name of goodness, you should deliberately choose to be one of them, and should be so enthusiastic over your work, puzzles me beyond all words. Don't say that you carry a black bag, and present cards which have to be filled up at the most inconvenient time; don't - "

He stopped suddenly, for the little girl was convulsed with laughter. She laughed until the tears rolled down her cheeks, and then she dried her eyes and laughed again.

"Excuse me," she said; "I can't help myself; it's so funny."

"It may be funny to you," he said, laughing in spite of himself; "but it is not funny to me."

"Of course it isn't," she replied, making a desperate effort to be serious. "Well, tell me something more about these tuners."

"Not another word," he said, gallantly. "I am ashamed

of myself as it is. Come to the end of the garden, and let me show you the view down into the valley."

She had conquered her fit of merriment, but her face wore a settled look of mischief, and she was evidently the possessor of some secret joke. She seemed in capital health and spirits, and had so much to say that was bright and interesting that Oswald Everard found himself becoming reconciled to the whole race of tuners. He was amazed to learn that she had walked all the way from Z -- , and quite alone, too.

"Oh, I don't think anything of that," she said; "I had a splendid time, and I caught four rare butterflies. I would not have missed those for anything. As for the going about by myself, that is a second nature. Besides, I do not belong to any one. That has its advantages, and I suppose its disadvantages; but at present I have only discovered the advantages. The disadvantages will discover themselves!"

"I believe you are what the novels call an advanced young woman," he said. "Perhaps you give lectures on woman's suffrage, or something of that sort?"

"I have very often mounted the platform," she answered. "In fact, I am never so happy as when addressing an immense audience. A most unfeminine thing to do, isn't it? What would the lady yonder in the horse-cloth dress and billycock hat say? Don't you think you ought to go and help her drive away the goat? She looks so frightened. She interests me deeply. I wonder whether she has written an essay on the feminine in woman. I should like to read it; it would do me so much good."

"You are at least a true woman," he said, laughing, "for I see you can be spiteful. The tuning has not driven that away."

"Ah, I had forgotten about the tuning," she answered, brightly; "but now you remind me, I have been seized with a great idea."

"Won't you tell it to me?" he asked.

"No," she answered; "I keep my great ideas for myself, and work them out in secret. And this one is particularly amusing. What fun I shall have!"

"But why keep the fun to yourself?" he said. "We all want to be amused here; we all want to be stirred up; a little fun would be a charity."

"Very well, since you wish it, you shall be stirred up," she answered; "but you must give me time to work out my great idea. I do not hurry about things, not even about my professional duties; for I have a strong feeling that it is vulgar to be always amassing riches! As I have neither a husband nor a brother to support, I have chosen less wealth, and more leisure to enjoy all the loveliness of life! So you see I take my time about everything. And to-morrow I shall catch butterflies at my leisure, and lie among the dear old pines, and work at my great idea."

"I shall catch butterflies," said her companion; "and I too shall lie among the dear old pines."

"Just as you please," she said; and at that moment the table d'hote bell rang.

The little girl hastened to the bureau, and spoke rapidly in German to the cashier.

"Ach, Fraulein!" he said. "You are not really serious?"

"Yes, I am," she said. "I don't want them to know my name. It will only worry me. Say I am the young lady who tuned the piano."

She had scarcely given these directions and mounted to her room when Oswald Everard, who was much interested in his mysterious companion, came to the bureau, and asked for the name of the little lady.

"Es ist das Fraulein welches das Piano gestimmt hat," answered the man, returning with unusual quickness to his account-book.

No one spoke to the little girl at table d'hote, but for all that she enjoyed her dinner, and gave her serious attention to all the courses. Being thus solidly occupied, she had not much leisure to bestow on the conversation of the other guests. Nor was it specially original; it treated of the short-comings of the chef, the tastelessness of the soup, the toughness of the beef, and all the many failings which go to complete a mountain hotel dinner. But suddenly, so it seemed to the little girl, this time-honoured talk passed into another phase; she heard the word "music" mentioned, and she became at once interested to learn what these people had to say on a subject which was dearer to her than any other.

"For my own part," said a stern-looking old man, "I have no words to describe what a gracious comfort music has been to me all my life. It is the noblest language which man may understand and speak. And I sometimes think that those who know it, or know something of it, are able at rare moments to find an answer to life's perplexing problems."

The little girl looked up from her plate. Robert Browning's words rose to her lips, but she did not give them utterance:

> God has a few of us whom He whispers in the ear;
> The rest may reason, and welcome; 'tis we musicians know.

"I have lived through a long life," said another elderly man, "and have therefore had my share of trouble; but the grief of being obliged to give up music was the grief which held me longest, or which perhaps has never left me. I still crave for the gracious pleasure of touching once more the strings of the violoncello, and hearing the dear, tender voice singing and throbbing, and answering even to such poor skill as mine. I still yearn to take my part in concerted music, and be one of those privileged to play Beethoven's string-quartettes. But that will have to be in another incarnation, I think."

He glanced at his shrunken arm, and then, as though ashamed of this allusion to his own personal infirmity, he added hastily:

"But when the first pang of such a pain is over, there remains the comfort of being a listener. At first one does not think it is a comfort; but as time goes on there is no resisting its magic influence. And Lowell said rightly that 'one of God's great charities is music.' "

"I did not know you were musical, Mr. Keith," said an English lady. "You have never before spoken of music."

"Perhaps not, madam," he answered. "One does not often speak of what one cares for most of all. But when I am in London I rarely miss hearing our best players."

At this point others joined in, and the various merits of eminent pianists were warmly discussed.

"What a wonderful name that little English lady has made for herself!" said the major, who was considered an authority on all subjects. I would go anywhere to hear Miss Thyra Flowerdew. We all ought to be very proud of her. She has taken even the German musical world by storm, and they say her recitals at Paris have been brilliantly successful. I myself have heard her at New York, Leipsic, London, Berlin, and even Chicago."

The little girl stirred uneasily in her chair.

"I don't think Miss Flowerdew has ever been to Chicago," she said.

There was a dead silence. The admirer of Miss Thyra Flowerdew looked much annoyed, and twiddled his watch-chain. He had meant to say "Philadelphia," but he did not think it necessary to own to his mistake.

"What impertinence!" said one of the ladies to Miss Blake. "What can she know about it? Is she not the young person who tuned the piano?"

"Perhaps she tunes Miss Thyra Flowerdew's piano!"

suggested Miss Blake, in a loud whisper.

"You are right, madam," said the little girl, quietly. "I have often tuned Miss Flowerdew's piano."

There was another embarrassing silence; and then a lovely old lady, whom every one reverenced, came to the rescue.

"I think her playing is simply superb," she said. "Nothing that I ever hear satisfies me so entirely. She has all the tenderness of an angel's touch."

"Listening to her," said the major, who had now recovered from his annoyance at being interrupted, "one becomes unconscious of her presence, for she is the music itself. And that is rare. It is but seldom nowadays that we are allowed to forget the personality of the player. And yet her personality is an unusual one; having once seen her, it would not be easy to forget her. I should recognise her anywhere."

As he spoke, he glanced at the little tuner, and could not help admiring her dignified composure under circumstances which might have been distressing to any one; and when she rose with the others he followed her, and said stiffly:

"I regret that I was the indirect cause of putting you in an awkward position."

"It is really of no consequence," she said, brightly. "If you think I was impertinent, I ask your forgiveness. I did not mean to be officious. The words were spoken before I was aware of them."

She passed into the salon, where she found a quiet corner for herself, and read some of the newspapers. No one took the slightest notice of her; not a word was spoken to her; but when she relieved the company of her presence her impertinence was commented on.

"I am sorry that she heard what I said," remarked Miss Blake; "but she did not seem to mind. These young women who go out into the world lose the edge of their sensitiveness and femininity. I have always observed that."

"How much they are spared then!" answered some one.

Meanwhile the little girl slept soundly. She had merry dreams, and finally woke up laughing. She hurried over her breakfast, and then stood ready to go for a butterfly hunt. She looked thoroughly happy, and evidently had found, and was holding tightly, the key to life's enjoyment.

Oswald Everard was waiting on the balcony, and he reminded her that he intended to go with her.

"Come along then," she answered; "we must not lose a moment."

They caught butterflies; they picked flowers; they ran; they lingered by the wayside; they sang; they climbed, and he marvelled at her easy speed. Nothing seemed to tire her, and everything seemed to delight her - the flowers, the birds, the clouds, the grasses, and the fragrance of the pine woods.

"Is it not good to live?" she cried. "Is it not splendid to take in the scented air? Draw in as many long breaths as you can. Isn't it good? Don't you feel now as though you were ready to move mountains? I do. What a dear old nurse Nature is! How she pets us, and gives us the best of her treasures!"

Her happiness invaded Oswald Everard's soul, and he felt like a school-boy once more, rejoicing in a fine day and his liberty, with nothing to spoil the freshness of the air, and nothing to threaten the freedom of the moment.

"Is it not good to live?" he cried. "Yes, indeed it is, if we know how to enjoy."

They had come upon some haymakers, and the little girl hastened up to help them, laughing and talking to the women, and helping them to pile up the hay on the shoulders of a broad-backed man, who then conveyed his burden to a pear-shaped stack. Oswald Everard watched his companion for a moment, and then, quite forgetting his dignity as an amateur tenor singer, he too lent his aid, and did not leave off until his companion sank exhausted on the ground.

"Oh," she laughed, "what delightful work for a very short time! Come along; let us go into that brown chatlet yonder and ask for some milk. I am simply parched with thirst. Thank you, but I prefer to carry my own flowers."

"What an independent little lady you are!" he said.

"It is quite necessary in our profession, I can assure you," she said, with a tone of mischief in her voice. "That reminds me that my profession is evidently not looked upon with any favour by the visitors at the hotel. I am heartbroken to think that I have not won the esteem of that lady in the billycock hat. What will she say to you for coming out with me? And what will she say of me for allowing you to come? I wonder whether she will say, 'How unfeminine!' I wish I could hear her!"

"I don't suppose you care," he said. "You seem to be a wild little bird."

"I don't care what a person of that description says," replied his companion.

"What on earth made you contradict the major at dinner last night?" he asked. "I was not at the table, but some one told me of the incident; and I felt very sorry about it. What could you know of Miss Thyra Flowerdew?"

"Well, considering that she is in my profession, of course I know something about her," said the little girl.

"Confound it all!" he said, rather rudely. "Surely there is some difference between the bellows-blower and the organist."

"Absolutely none," she answered; "merely a variation of the original theme!"

As she spoke she knocked at the door of the chalet, and asked the old dame to give them some milk. They sat in the Stube, and the little girl looked about, and admired the spinning-wheel and the quaint chairs and the queer old jugs and the pictures on the walls.

"Ah, but you shall see the other room," the old peasant

woman said; and she led them into a small apartment which was evidently intended for a study. It bore evidences of unusual taste and care, and one could see that some loving hand had been trying to make it a real sanctum of refinement. There was even a small piano. A carved book-rack was fastened to the wall.

The old dame did not speak at first; she gave her guests time to recover from the astonishment which she felt they must be experiencing; then she pointed proudly to the piano.

"I bought that for my daughters," she said, with a strange mixture of sadness and triumph. "I wanted to keep them at home with me, and I saved and saved, and got enough money to buy the piano. They had always wanted to have one, and I thought they would then stay with me. They liked music and books, and I knew they would be glad to have a room of their own where they might read and play and study; and so I gave them this corner."

"Well, mother," asked the little girl, "and where are they this afternoon?"

"Ah," she answered sadly, "they did not care to stay; but it was natural enough, and I was foolish to grieve. Besides, they come to see me."

"And then they play to you?" asked the little girl, gently.

"They say the piano is out of tune," the old dame said. "I don't know. Perhaps you can tell."

The little girl sat down to the piano, and struck a few chords.

"Yes," she said; "it is badly out of tune. Give me the tuning-hammer. I am sorry," she added, smiling at Oswald Everard, "but I cannot neglect my duty. Don't wait for me."

"I will wait for you," he said, sullenly; and he went into the balcony and smoked his pipe, and tried to possess his soul in patience.

When she had faithfully done her work she played a few simple melodies, such as she knew the old woman would love and understand; and she turned away when she saw that the listener's eyes were moist.

"Play once again," the old woman whispered. "I am dreaming of beautiful things."

So the little tuner touched the keys again with all the tenderness of an angel.

"Tell your daughters," she said, as she rose to say good-bye, "that the piano is now in good tune. Then they will play to you the next time they come."

"I shall always remember you, mademoiselle," the old woman said; and, almost unconsciously, she took the childish face and kissed it.

Oswald Everard was waiting in the hay-field for his companion; and when she apologised to him for this little professional intermezzo, as she called it, he recovered from his sulkiness and readjusted his nerves, which the noise of the tuning had somewhat disturbed.

"It was very good of you to tune the old dame's piano," he said, looking at her with renewed interest.

"Some one had to do it, of course," she answered, brightly, "and I am glad the chance fell to me. What a comfort it is to think that the next time those daughters come to see her they will play to her and make her very happy! Poor old dear!"

"You puzzle me greatly," he said. "I cannot for the life of me think what made you choose your calling. You must have many gifts; any one who talks with you must see that at once. And you play quite nicely, too."

"I am sorry that my profession sticks in your throat," she answered. "Do be thankful that I am nothing worse than a tuner. For I might be something worse - a snob, for instance."

And, so speaking, she dashed after a butterfly, and left him to recover from her words. He was conscious of having deserved a reproof; and when at last he overtook her he said as much, and asked for her kind indulgence.

"I forgive you," she said, laughing. "You and I are not looking at things from the same point of view; but we have had a splendid morning together, and I have enjoyed every minute of it. And to-morrow I go on my way."

"And to-morrow you go," he repeated. "Can it not be the day after to-morrow?"

"I am a bird of passage," she said, shaking her head. "You must not seek to detain me. I have taken my rest, and off I go to other climes."

They had arrived at the hotel, and Oswald Everard saw no more of his companion until the evening, when she came down rather late for table d'hote. She hurried over her dinner and went into the salon. She closed the door, and sat down to the piano, and lingered there without touching the keys; once or twice she raised her hands, and then she let them rest on the notes, and, half unconsciously, they began to move and make sweet music; and then they drifted into Schumann's "Abendlied," and then the little girl played some of his "Kinderscenen," and some of his "Fantasie Stucke," and some of his songs.

Her touch and feeling were exquisite, and her phrasing betrayed the true musician. The strains of music reached the dining-room, and, one by one, the guests came creeping in, moved by the music and anxious to see the musician.

The little girl did not look up; she was in a Schumann mood that evening, and only the players of Schumann know what enthralling possession he takes of their very spirit. All the passion and pathos and wildness and longing had found an inspired interpreter; and those who listened to her were held by the magic which was her own secret, and which had won for her such honour as comes only to the few. She understood Schumann's music, and was at her best with him.

Had she, perhaps, chosen to play his music this evening because she wished to be at her best? Or was she merely being impelled by an overwhelming force within her? Perhaps it was something of both.

Was she wishing to humiliate these people who had received her so coldly? This little girl was only human; perhaps there was something of that feeling too. Who can tell? But she played as she had never played in London, or Paris, or Berlin, or New York, or Philadelphia.

At last she arrived at the "Carnaval," and those who heard her declared afterward that they had never listened to a more magnificent rendering. The tenderness was so restrained; the vigour was so refined. When the last notes of that spirited "Marche des Davidsbundler contre les Philistins" had died away, she glanced at Oswald Everard, who was standing near her almost dazed.

"And now my favourite piece of all," she said; and she at once began the "Second Novelette," the finest of the eight, but seldom played in public.

What can one say of the wild rush of the leading theme, and the pathetic longing of the intermezzo?

> . . . The murmuring dying notes,
> That fall as soft as snow on the sea;

and

> The passionate strain that, deeply going,
> Refines the bosom it trembles through.

What can one say of those vague aspirations and finest thoughts which possess the very dullest among us when such music as that which the little girl had chosen catches us and keeps us, if only for a passing moment, but that moment of the rarest worth and loveliness in our unlovely lives?

What can one say of the highest music except that, like death, it is the great leveller: it gathers us all to its tender keeping - and we rest.

The little girl ceased playing. There was not a sound to be heard; the magic was still holding her listeners. When at last they had freed themselves with a sigh, they pressed forward to greet her.

"There is only one person who can play like that," cried the major, with sudden inspiration - "she is Miss Thyra Flowerdew."

The little girl smiled.

"That is my name," she said, simply; and she slipped out of the room.

The next morning, at an early hour, the bird of passage took her flight onward, but she was not destined to go off unobserved. Oswald Everard saw the little figure swinging along the road, and she overtook her.

"You little wild bird!" he said. "And so this was your great idea - to have your fun out of us all, and then play to us and make us feel I don't know how, and then to go."

"You said the company wanted stirring up," she answered, "and I rather fancy I have stirred them up."

"And what do you suppose you have done for me?" he asked.

"I hope I have proved to you that the bellows-blower and the organist are sometimes identical," she answered.

But he shook his head.

"Little wild bird," he said, "you have given me a great idea, and I will tell you what it is: to tame you. So good-bye for the present."

"Good-bye," she said. "But wild birds are not so easily tamed."

Then she waved her hand over her head, and went on her way singing.

## KOOSJE: A STUDY OF DUTCH LIFE

Her name was Koosje van Kampen, and she lived in Utrecht, that most quaint of quaint cities, the Venice of the North.

All her life had been passed under the shadow of the grand old Dom Kerk; she had played bo-peep behind the columns and arcades of the ruined, moss-grown cloisters; had slipped up and fallen down the steps leading to the grachts; had once or twice, in this very early life, been fished out of those same slimy, stagnant waters; had wandered under the great lindens in the Baan, and gazed curiously up at the stork's nest in the tree by the Veterinary School; had pattered about the hollow-sounding streets in her noisy wooden klompen; had danced and laughed, had quarrelled and wept, and fought and made friends again, to the tune of the silver chimes high up in the Dom - chimes that were sometimes old Nederlandsche hymns, sometimes Mendelssohn's melodies and tender "Lieder ohne Worte."

But that was ever so long ago, and now she had left her romping childhood behind her, and had become a maid-servant - a very dignified and aristocratic maid-servant indeed - with no less a sum than eight pounds ten a year in wages.

She lived in the house of a professor, who dwelt on the

Munster Kerkhoff, one of the most aristocratic parts of that wonderfully aristocratic city; and once or twice every week you might have seen her, if you had been there to see, busily engaged in washing the red tile and blue slate pathway in front of the professor's house. You would have seen that she was very pleasant to look at, this Koosje, very comely and clean, whether she happened to be very busy, or whether it had been Sunday, and, with her very best gown on, she was out for a promenade in the Baan, after duly going to service as regularly as the Sabbath dawned in the grand old Gothic choir of the cathedral.

During the week she wore always the same costume as does every other servant in the country: a skirt of black stuff, short enough to show a pair of very neat-set and well-turned ankles, clad in cloth shoes and knitted stockings that showed no wrinkles; over the skirt a bodice and a kirtle of lilac, made with a neatly gathered frilling about her round brown throat; above the frilling five or six rows of unpolished garnet beads fastened by a massive clasp of gold filigree, and on her head a spotless white cap tied with a neat bow under her chin - as neat, let me tell you, as an Englishman's tie at a party.

But it was on Sunday that Koosje shone forth in all the glory of a black gown and her jewellery - with great ear-rings to match the clasp of her necklace, and a heavy chain and cross to match that again, and one or two rings; while on her head she wore an immense cap, much too big to put a bonnet over, though for walking she was most particular to have gloves.

Then, indeed, she was a young person to be treated with respect, and with respect she was undoubtedly treated. As she passed along the quaint, resounding streets, many a head was turned to look after her; but Koosje went on her way like the staid maiden she was, duly impressed with the fact that she was principal servant of Professor van Dijck, the most celebrated authority on the study of osteology in Europe. So Koosje never heeded the looks, turned her head neither to the right nor to the left, but went sedately on her business or pleasure, whichever it happened to be.

It was not likely that such a treasure could remain long unnoticed and unsought after. Servants in the Netherlands, I hear, are not so good but that they might be better; and most people knew what a treasure Professor van Dijck had in his Koosje. However, as the professor conscientiously raised her wages from time to time, Koosje never thought of leaving him.

But there is one bribe no woman can resist - the bribe that is offered by love. As Professor van Dijck had expected and feared, that bribe ere long was held out to Koosje, and Koosje was too weak to resist it. Not that he wished her to do so. If the girl had a chance of settling well and happily for life, he would be the last to dream of throwing any obstacle in her way. He had come to be an old man himself; he lived all alone, save for his servants, in a great, rambling house, whose huge apartments were all set out with horrible anatomical preparations and grisly skeletons; and, though the stately passages were paved with white marble, and led into rooms which would easily have accommodated crowds of guests, he went into no society save that of savants as old and fossil-like as himself; in other words, he was an old bachelor who lived entirely for his profession and the study of the great masters by the interpretation of a genuine old

Stradivari. Yet the old professor had a memory; he recalled the time when he had been young who now was old - the time when his heart was a good deal more tender, his blood a great deal warmer, and his fancy very much more easily stirred than nowadays. There was a dead-and-gone romance which had broken his heart, sentimentally speaking - a romance long since crumbled into dust, which had sent him for comfort into the study of osteology and the music of the Stradivari; yet the memory thereof made him considerably more lenient to Koosje's weakness than Koosje herself had ever expected to find him.

Not that she had intended to tell him at first; she was only three and twenty, and, though Jan van der Welde was as fine a fellow as could be seen in Utrecht, and had good wages and something put by, Koosje was by no means inclined to rush headlong into matrimony with undue hurry. It was more pleasant to live in the professor's good house, to have delightful walks arm in arm with Jan under the trees in the Baan or round the Singels, parting under the stars with many a lingering word and promise to meet again. It was during one of those very partings that the professor suddenly became aware, as he walked placidly home, of the change that had come into Koosje's life.

However, Koosje told him blushingly that she did not wish to leave him just at present; so he did not trouble himself about the matter. He was a wise man, this old authority on osteology, and quoted oftentimes, "Sufficient unto the day is the evil thereof."

So the courtship sped smoothly on, seeming for once to contradict the truth of the old saying, "The course of true love never did run smooth." The course of their love did, of a truth, run marvellously smooth indeed. Koosje, if a trifle coy, was pleasant and sweet; Jan as fine a fellow as ever waited round a corner on a cold winter night. So brightly the happy days slipped by, when suddenly a change was effected in the professor's household which made, as a matter of course, somewhat of a change in Koosje's life. It came about in this wise.

Koosje had been on an errand for the professor, - one that had kept her out of doors some time, - and it happened that the night was bitterly cold; the cold, indeed, was fearful. The air had that damp rawness so noticeable in Dutch climate, a thick mist overhung the city, and a drizzling rain came down with a steady persistence such as quickly soaked through the stoutest and thickest garments. The streets were well-nigh empty. The great thoroughfare, the Oude Gracht, was almost deserted, and as Koosje hurried along the Meinerbroederstraat - for she had a second commission there - she drew her great shawl more tightly round her, muttering crossly, "What weather! yesterday so warm, to-day so cold. 'Tis enough to give one the fever."

She delivered her message, and ran on through Oude Kerkhoff as fast as her feet could carry her, when, just as she turned the corner into the Domplein, a fierce gust of wind, accompanied by a blinding shower of rain, assailed her; her foot caught against something soft and heavy, and she fell.

"Bless us!" she ejaculated, blankly. "What fool has left a bundle out on the path on such a night? Pitch dark, with half the lamps out, and rain and mist enough to blind one."

She gathered herself up, rubbing elbows and knees vigorously, casting the while dark glances at the obnoxious bundle which had caused the disaster. Just then the wind was lulled, the lamp close at hand gave out a steady light, which shed its rays through the fog upon Koosje and the bundle, from which, to the girl's horror and dismay, came a faint moan. Quickly she drew nearer, when she perceived that what she had believed to be a bundle was indeed a woman, apparently in the last stage of exhaustion.

Koosje tried to lift her; but the dead-weight was beyond her, young and strong as she was. Then the rain and the wind came on again in fiercer gusts than before; the woman's moans grew louder and louder, and what to do Koosje knew not.

She struggled on for the few steps that lay between her and the professor's house, and then she rang a peal which resounded through the echoing passages, bringing Dortje, the other maid, running out; after the manner of her class, imagining all sorts of terrible catastrophes had happened. She uttered a cry of relief when she perceived it was only Koosje, who, without vouchsafing any explanation, dashed past her and ran straight into the professor's room.

"O professor!" she gasped out; but, between her efforts to remove the woman, her struggle with the elements, and her race down the passage, her breath was utterly gone.

The professor looked up from his book and his tea-tray in surprise. For a moment he thought that Koosje, his domestic treasure, had altogether taken leave of her senses; for she was streaming with water, covered with mud, and head and cap were in a state of disorder, such as neither he nor any one else had ever seen them in since the last time she had been fished out of the Nieuwe Gracht. "What is the matter, Koosje?" he asked, regarding her gravely over his spectacles.

"There's a woman outside - dying," she panted, "I fell over her."

"You had better try to get her in then," the old gentleman said, in quite a relieved tone. "You and Dortje must bring her in. Dear, dear, poor soul! but it is a dreadful night."

The old gentleman shivered as he spoke, and drew a little nearer to the tall white porcelain stove.

It was, as he had said a minute before, a terrible night. He could hear the wind beating about the house and rattling about the casements and moaning down the chimneys; and to think any poor soul should be out on such a night, dying! Heaven preserve others who might be belated or houseless in any part of the world!

He fell into a fit of abstraction, - a habit not uncommon with learned men, - wondering why life should be so different with different people; why he should be in that warm, handsome room, with its soft rich hangings and carpet, with its beautiful furniture of carved wood, its pictures, and the rare china scattered here and there among the grim array of skeletons which were his delight. He wondered why he should take his tea out of costly and valuable Oriental china, sugar and cream out of antique silver, while other poor souls had no tea at all, and nothing to take it out of even if they had. He wondered why he should have a lamp under his teapot that was a very marvel of art transparencies; why he should have every luxury, and this poor creature should be dying in the street amid the wind and the rain. It was all very unequal.

It was very odd, the professor argued, leaning his back against the tall, warm stove; it was very odd indeed. He began to feel that, grand as the study of osteology undoubtedly is, he ought not to permit it to become so engrossing as to blind him to the study of the greater philosophies of life. His reverie was, however, broken by the abrupt reentrance of Koosje, who this time was a trifle less breathless than she had been before.

"We have got her into the kitchen, professor," she announced. "She is a child - a mere baby, and so pretty! She has opened her eyes and spoken."

"Give her some soup and wine - hot," said the professor, without stirring.

"But won't you come?" she asked.

The professor hesitated; he hated attending in cases of illness, though he was a properly qualified doctor and in an emergency would lay his prejudice aside.

"Or shall I run across for the good Dr. Smit?" Koosje asked. "He would come in a minute, only it is such a night!"

At that moment a fiercer gust than before rattled at the casements, and the professor laid aside his scruples.

He followed his housekeeper down the chilly, marble-flagged passage into the kitchen, where he never went for months together - a cosey enough, pleasant place, with a deep valance hanging from the mantel-shelf, with many great copper pans, bright and shining as new gold, and furniture all scrubbed to the whiteness of snow.

In an arm-chair before the opened stove sat the rescued girl - a slight, golden-haired thing, with wistful blue eyes and a frightened air. Every moment she caught her breath in a half-hysterical sob, while violent shivers shook her from head to foot.

The professor went and looked at her over his spectacles, as if she had been some curious specimen of his favourite study; but at the same time he kept at a respectful distance from her.

"Give her some soup and wine," he said, at length, putting his hands under the tails of his long dressing-gown of flowered cashmere. "Some soup and wine - hot; and put her to bed."

"Is she then to remain for the night?" Koosje asked, a little surprised.

"Oh, don't send me away!" the golden-haired girl broke out, in a voice that was positively a wail, and clasping a pair of pretty, slender hands in piteous supplication.

"Where do you come from?" the old gentleman asked, much as if he expected she might suddenly jump up and bite him.

"From Beijerland, mynheer," she answered, with a sob.

"So! Koosje, she is remarkably well dressed, is she

not?" the professor said, glancing at the costly lace head-gear, the heavy gold head-piece, which lay on the table together with the great gold spiral ornaments and filigree pendants - a dazzling head of richness. He looked, too, at the girl's white hands, at the rich, crape-laden gown, at their delicate beauty, and shower of waving golden hair, which, released from the confinement of the cap and head-piece, floated in a rich mass of glittering beauty over the pillows which his servant had placed beneath her head.

The professor was old; the professor was wholly given up to his profession, which he jokingly called his sweetheart; and, though he cut half of his acquaintances in the street through inattention and the shortness of his sight, he had eyes in his head, and upon occasions could use them. He therefore repeated the question.

"Very well dressed indeed, professor," returned Koosje, promptly.

"And what are you doing in Utrecht - in such a plight as this, too?" he asked, still keeping at a safe distance.

"O mynheer, I am all alone in the world," she answered, her blue misty eyes filled with tears. "I had a month ago a dear, good, kind father, but he has died, and I am indeed desolate. I always believed him rich, and to these things," with a gesture that included her dress and the ornaments on the table, "I have ever been accustomed. Thus I ordered without consideration such clothes as I thought needful. And then I found there was nothing for me - not a hundred guilders to call my own when all was paid."

"But what brought you to Utrecht?"

"He sent me here, mynheer. In his last illness, only of three days' duration, he bade me gather all together and come to this city, where I was to ask for a Mevrouw Baake, his cousin."

"Mevrouw Baake, of the Sigaren Fabrijk," said Dortje, in an aside, to the others. "I lived servant with her before I came here."

"I had heard very little about her, only my father had sometimes mentioned his cousin to me; they had once been betrothed," the stranger continued. "But when I reached Utrecht I found she was dead - two years dead; but we had never heard of it."

"Dear, dear, dear!" exclaimed the professor, pityingly. "Well, you had better let Koosje put you to bed, and we will see what can be done for you in the morning."

"Am I to make up a bed?" Koosje asked, following him along the passage.

The professor wheeled round and faced her.

"She had better sleep in the guest room," he said, thoughtfully, regardless of the cold which struck to his slippered feet from the marble floor. "That is the only room which does not contain specimens that would probably frighten the poor child. I am very much afraid, Koosje," he concluded, doubtfully, "that she is a lady; and what we are to do with a lady I can't think."

With that the old gentleman shuffled off to his cosey room, and Koosje turned back to her kitchen.

"He'll never think of marrying her," mused Koosje, rather blankly. If she had spoken the thoughts to the professor himself, she would have received a very emphatic assurance that, much as the study of osteology and the Stradivari had blinded him to the affairs of this workaday world, he was not yet so thoroughly foolish as to join his fossilised wisdom to the ignorance of a child of sixteen or seventeen.

However, on the morrow matters assumed a somewhat different aspect. Gertrude van Floote proved to be not exactly a gentlewoman. It is true that her father had been a well-to-do man for his station in life, and had very much spoiled and indulged his one motherless child. Yet her education was so slight that she could do little more than read and write, besides speaking a little English, which she had picked up from the yachtsmen frequenting her native town. The professor found she had been but a distant relative of the Mevrouw Baake, to seek whom she had come to Utrecht, and that she had no kinsfolk upon whom she could depend - a fact which accounted for the profusion of her jewellery, all her golden trinkets having descended to her as heirlooms.

"I can be your servant, mynheer," she suggested. "Indeed, I am a very useful girl, as you will find if you will but try me."

Now, as a rule, the professor vigorously set his face against admitting young servants into his house. They broke his china, they disarranged his bones, they meddled with his papers, and made general havoc. So, in truth, he was not very willing to have Gertrude van Floote as a permanent member of his household, and he said so.

But Koosje had taken a fancy to the girl; and having an eye to her own departure at no very distant date, - for she had been betrothed more than two years, - she pleaded so hard to keep her, promising to train her in all the professor's ways, to teach her the value of old china and osteologic specimens, that eventually, with a good deal of grumbling, the old gentleman gave way, and, being a wise as well as an old gentleman, went back to his studies, dismissing Koosje and the girl alike from his thoughts.

Just at first Truide, poor child, was charmed.

She put away her splendid ornaments, and some lilac frocks and black skirts were purchased for her. Her box, which she had left at the station, supplied all that was necessary for Sunday.

It was great fun! For a whole week this young person danced about the rambling old house, playing at being a servant. Then she began to grow a little weary of it all. She had been accustomed, of course, to performing such offices as all Dutch ladies fulfil - the care of china, of linen, the dusting of rooms, and the like; but she had done them as a mistress, not as an underling. And that was not the worst; it was when it came to her pretty feet having to be thrust into klompen, and her having to take a pail and syringe and mop and clean the windows and the pathway and the front of the house, that the game of maid-servant began to assume a very different aspect. When, after having been as free as air to come and go as she chose, she was only permitted to attend service on Sundays, and to take an hour's promenade with Dortje, who was dull and heavy and stupid, she began to feel positively desperate; and the result of it all was that when Jan van der Welde came, as he was accustomed to do nearly every evening, to see Koosje, Miss Truide, from sheer longing for excitement and change, began to make eyes at him, with what effect I will endeavour to show.

Just at first Koosje noticed nothing. She herself was of so faithful a nature that an idea, a suspicion, of Jan's faithlessness never entered her mind. When the girl laughed and blushed and dimpled and smiled, when she cast her great blue eyes at the big young fellow, Koosje only thought how pretty she was, and it was must a thousand pities she had not been born a great lady.

And thus weeks slipped over. Never very demonstrative herself, Koosje saw nothing, Dortje, for her part, saw a great deal; but Dortje was a woman of few words, one who quite believed in the saying, "If speech is silver, silence is gold;" so she held her peace.

Now Truide, rendered fairly frantic by her enforced confinement to the house, grew to look upon Jan as her only chance of excitement and distraction; and Jan, poor, thick-headed noodle of six feet high, was thoroughly wretched. What to do he knew not. A strange, mad, fierce passion for Truide had taken possession of him, and an utter distaste, almost dislike, had come in place of the old love for Koosje. Truide was unlike anything he had ever come in contact with before; she was so fairy-like, so light, so delicate, so dainty. Against Koosje's plumper, maturer charms, she appeared to the infatuated young man like - if he had ever heard of it he would probably have said like a Dresden china image; but since he had not, he compared her in his own foolish heart to an angel. Her feet were so tiny, her hands so soft, her eyes so expressive, her waist so slim, her manner so bewitching! Somehow Koosje was altogether different; he could not endure the touch of her heavy hand, the tones of her less refined voice; he grew impatient at the denser perceptions of her mind. It was very foolish, very short-sighted; for the hands, though heavy, were clever and willing; the voice, though a trifle coarser in accent than Truide's childish tones, would never tell him a lie; the perceptions, though not brilliant, were the perceptions of good, every-day common sense. It really was very foolish, for what charmed him most in Truide was the merest outside polish, a certain ease of manner which doubtless she had caught from the English aristocrats whom she had known in her native place. She had not half the sterling good qualities and steadfastness of Koosje; but Jan was in love, and did not stop to argue the matter as you or I are able to do. Men in love - very wise and great men, too - are often like Jan van der Welde. They lay aside pro tem. the whole amount, be it great or small, of wisdom they possess. And it must be remembered that Jan van der Welde was neither a wise nor a great man.

Well, in the end there came what the French call un denouement, - what we in forcible modern English would call a smash, - and it happened thus. It was one evening toward the summer that Koosje's eyes were suddenly opened, and she became aware of the free-and-easy familiarity of Truide's manner toward her betrothed lover, Jan. It was some very slight and trivial thing that led her to notice it, but in an instant the whole truth flashed across her mind.

"Leave the kitchen!" she said, in a tone of authority.

But it happened that, at the very instant she spoke, Jan

was furtively holding Truide's fingers under the cover of the table-cloth; and when, on hearing the sharp words, the girl would have snatched them away, he, with true masculine instinct of opposition, held them fast.

"What do you mean by speaking to her like that?" he demanded, an angry flush overspreading his dark face.

"What is the maid to you?" Koosje asked, indignantly.

"Maybe more than you are," he retorted; in answer to which Koosje deliberately marched out of the kitchen, leaving them alone.

To say she was indignant would be but very mildly to express the state of her feelings; she was furious. She knew that the end of her romance had come. No thoughts of making friends with Jan entered her mind; only a great storm filled her heart till it was ready to burst with pain and anguish.

As she went along the passage the professor's bell sounded, and Koosje, being close to the door, went abruptly in. The professor looked up in mild astonishment, quickly enough changed to dismay as he caught sight of his valued Koosje's face, from out of which anger seemed in a moment to have thrust all the bright, comely beauty.

"How now, my good Koosje?" said the old gentleman. "Is aught amiss?"

"Yes, professor, there is," returned Koosje, all in a blaze of anger, and moving, as she spoke, the tea-tray, which she set down upon the oaken buffet with a bang, which made its fair and delicate freight fairly jingle again.

"But you needn't break my china, Koosje," suggested the old gentleman, mildly, rising from his chair and getting into his favourite attitude before the stove.

"You are quite right, professor," returned Koosje, curtly; she was sensible even in her trouble.

"And what is the trouble?" he asked, gently.

"It's just this, professor," cried Koosje, setting her arms akimbo and speaking in a high-pitched, shrill voice; "you and I have been warming a viper in our bosoms, and, viper-like, she has turned round and bitten me."

"Is it Truide?"

"Truide," she affirmed, disdainfully. "Yes, it is Truide, who but for me would be dead now of hunger and cold - or worse. And she has been making love to that great fool, Jan van der Welde, - great oaf that he is, - after all I have done for her; after my dragging her in out of the cold and rain; after all I have taught her. Ah, professor, but it is a vile, venomous viper that we have been warming in our bosoms!"

"I must beg, Koosje," said the old gentleman, sedately, "that you will exonerate me from any such proceeding. If you remember rightly, I was altogether against your plan for keeping her in the house." He could not resist giving her that little dig, kind of heart as he was.

"Serves me right for being so soft-hearted!" thundered Koosje. "I'll be wiser next time I fall over a bundle, and leave it where I find it."

"No, no, Koosje; don't say that," the old gentleman remonstrated, gently. "After all, it may be but a blessing in disguise. God sends all our trials for some good and wise purpose. Our heaviest afflictions are often, nay, most times, Koosje, means to some great end which, while the cloud of adversity hangs over us, we are unable to discern."

"Ah!" sniffed Koosje, scornfully.

"This oaf - as I must say you justly term him, for you are a good clever woman, Koosje, as I can testify after the experience of years - has proved that he can be false; he has shown that he can throw away substance for shadow (for, of a truth, that poor, pretty child would make a sad wife for a poor man); yet it is better you should know it now than at some future date, when - when there might be other ties to make the knowledge more bitter to you."

"Yes, that is true," said Koosje, passing the back of her hand across her trembling lips. She could not shed tears over her trouble; her eyes were dry and burning, as if anger had scorched the blessed drops up ere they should fall. She went on washing up the cups and saucers, or at least the cup and saucer, and other articles the professor had used for his tea; and after a few minutes' silence he spoke again.

"What are you going to do? Punish her, or turn her out, or what?"

"I shall let him - marry her," replied Koosje, with a portentous nod.

The old gentleman couldn't help laughing. "You think he will pay off your old scores?"

"Before long," answered Koosje, grimly, "she will find him out - as I have done."

Then, having finished washing the tea-things, which the professor had shuddered to behold in her angry hands, she whirled herself out of the room and left him alone.

"Oh, these women - these women!" he cried, in confidence, to the pictures and skeletons. "What a worry they are! An old bachelor has the best of it in the main, I do believe. But oh, Jan van der Welde, what a donkey you must be to get yourself mixed up in such a broil! and yet - ah!"

The fossilised old gentleman broke off with a sigh as he recalled the memory of a certain dead-and-gone romance which had happened – goodness only knows how many years before - when he, like Jan van der Welde, would have thrown the world away for a glance of a certain pair of blue eyes, at the bidding of a certain English tongue, whose broken Nederlandsche taal was to him the sweetest music ever heard on earth - sweeter even than the strains of the Stradivari when from under his skilful fingers rose the perfect melodies of old masters. Ay, but the sweet eyes had been closed in death many a long, long, year, the sweet voice hushed in silence. He had watched the dear life ebb away, the fire in the blue eyes fade out. He had felt each day that the clasp of the little greeting fingers was less close; each day he had seen the outline of the face grow sharper; and at last there had come one when the poor little English-woman met him with the gaze of one who knew him not, and babbled, not of green fields, but of horses and dogs, and of a brother Jack, who, five years before, had gone down with her Majesty's ship Alligator in mid-Atlantic.

Ay, but that was many and many a year agone. His young, blue-eyed love stood out alone in life's history, a thing apart. Of the gentler sex, in a general way, the old professor had not seen that which had raised it in his estimation to the level of the one woman over whose memory hung a bright halo of romance.

Fifteen years had passed away; the old professor of osteology had passed away with them; and in the large house on the Domplein lived a baron, with half a dozen noisy, happy, healthy children, - young fraulas and jonkheers, - who scampered up and down the marble passages, and fell headlong down the steep, narrow, unlighted stairways, to the imminent danger of dislocating their aristocratic little necks. There was a new race of neat maids, clad in the same neat livery of lilac and black, who scoured and cleaned, just as Koosje and Dortje had done in the old professor's day. You might, indeed, have heard the selfsame names resounding through the echoing rooms: "Koos-je! Dort-je!"

But the Koosje and Dortje were not the same. What had become of Dortje I cannot say; but on the left-hand side of the busy, bustling, picturesque Oude Gracht there was a handsome shop filled with all manner of cakes, sweeties, confections, and liquors - from absinthe to Benedictine, or arrack to chartreuse. In that shop was a handsome, prosperous, middle-aged woman, well dressed and well mannered, no longer Professor van Dijck's Koosje, but the

Jevrouw van Kampen.

Yes; Koosje had come to be a prosperous tradeswoman of good position, respected by all. But she was Koosje van Kampen still; the romance which had come to so disastrous and abrupt an end had sufficed for her life. Many an offer had been made to her, it is true; but she had always declared that she had had enough of lovers - she had found out their real value.

I must tell you that at the time of Jan's infidelity, after the first flush of rage was over, Koosje disdained to show any sign of grief or regret. She was very proud, this Netherland servant-maid, far too proud to let those by whom she was surrounded imagine she was wearing the willow for the faithless Jan; and when Dortje, on the day of the wedding, remarked that for her part she had always considered Koosje remarkably cool on the subject of matrimony, Koosje with a careless out-turning of her hands, palms uppermost, answered that she was right.

Very soon after their marriage Jan and his young wife left Utrecht for Arnheim, where Jan had promise of higher wages; and thus they passed, as Koosje thought, completely out of her life.

"I don't wish to hear anything more about them, if - you - please," she said, severely and emphatically, to Dortje.

But not so. In time the professor died, leaving Koosje the large legacy with which she set up the handsome shop in the Oude Gracht; and several years passed on.

It happened one day that Koosje was sitting in her shop

sewing. In the large inner room a party of ladies and officers were eating cakes and drinking chocolates and liquors with a good deal of fun and laughter, when the door opened timidly, thereby letting in a gust of bitter wind, and a woman crept fearfully in, followed by two small, crying children.

Could the lady give her something to eat? she asked; they had had nothing during the day, and the little ones were almost famished.

Koosje, who was very charitable, lifted a tray of large, plain buns, and was about to give her some, when her eyes fell upon the poor beggar's faded face, and she exclaimed:

"Truide!"

Truide, for it was she, looked up in startled surprise.

"I did not know, or I would not have come in, Koosje," she said, humbly; "for I treated you very badly."

"Ve-ry bad-ly," returned Koosje, emphatically. "Then where is Jan?"

"Dead!" murmured Truide, sadly.

"Dead! so - ah, well! I suppose I must do something for you. Here Yanke!" opening the door and calling, "Yanke!"

"Je, jevrouw," a voice cried, in reply.

The next moment a maid came running into the shop.

"Take these people into the kitchen and give them something to eat. Put them by the stove while you prepare it. There is some soup and that smoked ham we had for koffy. Then come here and take my place for a while."

"Je, jevrouw," said Yanke, disappearing again, followed by Truide and her children.

Then Koosje sat down again, and began to think.

"I said," she mused, presently, "that night that the next time I fell over a bundle I'd leave it where I found it. Ah, well! I'm not a barbarian; I couldn't do that. I never thought, though, it would be Truide."

"Hi, jevrouw," was called from the inner room.

"Je, mynheer," jumping up and going to her customers.

She attended to their wants, and presently bowed them out.

"I never thought it would be Truide," she repeated to herself, as she closed the door behind the last of the gay uniforms and jingling scabbards. "And Jan is dead - ah, well!"

Then she went into the kitchen, where the miserable children - girls both of them, and pretty had they been clean and less forlornly clad - were playing about the stove.

"So Jan is dead," began Koosje, seating herself.

"Yes, Jan is dead," Truide answered.

"And he left you nothing?" Koosje asked.

"We had had nothing for a long time," Truide replied, in her sad, crushed voice. "We didn't get on very well; he soon got tired of me."

"That was a weakness of his," remarked Koosje, drily.

"We lost five little ones, one after another," Truide continued. "And Jan was fond of them, and somehow it seemed to sour him. As for me, I was sorry enough at the time, Heaven knows, but it was as well. But Jan said it seemed as if a curse had fallen upon us; he began to wish you back again, and to blame me for having come between you. And then he took to genever, and then to wish for something stronger; so at last every stiver went for absinthe, and once or twice he beat me, and then he died."

"Just as well," muttered Koosje, under her breath.

"It is very good of you to have fed and warmed us," Truide went on, in her faint, complaining tones. "Many a one would have let me starve, and I should have deserved it. It is very good of you and we are grateful; but 'tis time we were going, Koosje and Mina;" then added, with a shake of her head, "but I don't know where."

"Oh, you'd better stay," said Koosje, hurriedly. "I live in this big house by myself, and I dare say you'll be more useful in the shop than Yanke - if your tongue is as glib as it used to be, that is. You know some English, too, don't you?"

"A little," Truide answered, eagerly.

"And after all," Koosje said, philosophically, shrugging her shoulders, "you saved me from the beatings and the starvings and the rest. I owe you something for that. Why, if it hadn't been for you I should have been silly enough to have married him."

And then she went back to her shop, saying to herself:

"The professor said it was a blessing in disguise; God sends all our trials to work some great purpose. Yes; that was what he said, and he knew most things. Just think if I were trailing about now with those two little ones, with nothing to look back to but a schnapps-drinking husband who beat me! Ah, well, well! things are best as they are. I don't know that I ought not to be very much obliged to her - and she'll be very useful in the shop."

## A DOG OF FLANDERS

Nello and Patrasche were left all alone in the world.

They were friends in a friendship closer than brotherhood. Nello was a little Ardennois; Patrasche was a big Fleming. They were both of the same age by length of years; yet one was still young, and the other was already old. They had dwelt together almost all their days; both were orphaned and destitute, and owed their lives to the same hand. It had been the beginning of the tie between them, - their first bond of sympathy, - and it had strengthened day by day, and had grown with their growth, firm and indissoluble, until they loved one another very greatly.

Their home was a little hut on the edge of a little village - a Flemish village a league from Antwerp, set amidst flat breadths of pasture and corn-lands, with long lines of poplars and of alders bending in the breeze on the edge of the great canal which ran through it. It had about a score of houses and homesteads, with shutters of bright green or sky blue, and roofs rose red or black and white, and walls whitewashed until they shone in the sun like snow. In the centre of the village stood a windmill, placed on a little moss-grown slope; it was a landmark to all the level country round. It had once been painted scarlet, sails and all; but that had been in its infancy, half a century or more earlier, when it had ground wheat for the soldiers of Napoleon; and it was now a ruddy brown, tanned by wind and weather. It went queerly by fits and starts, as though rheumatic and stiff in the joints from age; but it served the whole neighborhood, which would have thought it almost as impious to carry grain elsewhere as to attend any other religious service than the mass that was performed at the altar of the little old gray church, with its conical steeple, which stood opposite to it, and whose single bell rang morning, noon, and night with that strange, subdued, hollow sadness which every bell that hangs in the Low Countries seems to gain as an integral part of its melody.

Within sound of the little melancholy clock almost from their birth upward, they had dwelt together, Nello and Patrasche, in the little hut on the edge of the village, with the cathedral spire of Antwerp rising in the northeast, beyond the great green plain of seeding grass and spreading corn that stretched away from them like a tideless, changeless sea. It was the hut of a very old man, of a very poor man - of old Jehan Daas, who in his time had been a soldier, and who remembered the wars that had trampled the country as oxen tread down the furrows, and who had brought from his service nothing except a wound, which had made him a cripple.

When old Jehan Daas had reached his full eighty, his daughter had died in the Ardennes, hard by Stavelot, and had left him in legacy her two-year-old son. The old man could ill contrive to support himself, but he took up the additional burden uncomplainingly, and it soon became welcome and precious to him. Little Nello, which was but a pet diminutive for Nicolas, throve with him, and the old man and the little child lived in the poor little hut contentedly.

It was a very humble little mud hut indeed, but it was clean and white as a sea-shell, and stood in a small plot of garden ground that yielded beans and herbs and pumpkins. They were very poor, terribly poor; many a day they had nothing at all to eat. They never by any chance had enough; to have had enough to eat would have been to have reached paradise at once. But the old man was very gentle and good to the boy, and the boy was a beautiful, innocent, truthful, tender-natured creature; and they were happy on a crust and a few leaves of cabbage, and asked no more of earth or heaven - save indeed that Patrasche should be always with them, since without Patrasche where would they have been?

For Patrasche was their alpha and omega; their treasury and granary; their store of gold and wand of wealth; their bread-winner and minister; their only friend and comforter. Patrasche dead or gone from them, they must have laid themselves down and died likewise. Patrasche was body, brains, hands, head, and feet to both of them; Patrasche was their very life, their very soul. For Jehan Daas was old and a cripple, and Nello was but a child; and Patrasche was their dog.

A dog of Flanders - yellow of hide, large of head and limb, with wolf-like ears that stood erect, and legs bowed and feet widened in the muscular development wrought in his breed by many generations of hard service. Patrasche came of a race which had toiled hard and cruelly from sire to son in Flanders many a century - slaves of slaves, dogs of the people, beasts of the shafts and the harness, creatures that lived straining their sinews in the gall of the cart, and died breaking their hearts on the flints of the streets.

Patrasche had been born of parents who had labored hard all their days over the sharp-set stones of the various cities and the long, shadowless, weary roads of the two Flanders and of Brabant. He had been born to no other heritage than those of pain and of toil. He had been fed on curses and baptized with blows. Why not? It was a Christian country, and Patrasche was but a dog. Before he was fully grown he had known the bitter gall of the cart and the collar. Before he had entered his thirteenth month he had become the property of a hardware dealer, who was accustomed to wander over the land north and south, from the blue sea to the green mountains. They sold him for a small price, because he was so young.

This man was a drunkard and a brute. The life of Patrasche was a life of hell. To deal the tortures of hell on the animal creation is a way which the Christians have of showing their belief in it. His purchaser was a sullen, ill-living, brutal Brabantois, who heaped his cart full with pots and pans and flagons and buckets, and other wares of crockery and brass and tin, and left Patrasche to draw the load as best he might, while he himself lounged idly by the side in fat and sluggish ease, smoking his black pipe and stopping at every wineshop or cafe on the road.

Happily for Patrasche, or unhappily, he was very strong; he came of an iron race, long born and bred to such cruel travail; so that he did not die, but managed to drag on a wretched existence under the brutal burdens, the scarifying lashes, the hunger, the thirst, the blows, the curses, and the exhaustion which are the only wages with which the Flemings repay the most patient and laborious of all their four-footed victims. One day, after two years of this long and deadly agony, Patrasche was going on as usual along one of the straight, dusty, unlovely roads that lead to the city of Rubens. It was full midsummer, and very warm. His cart was very heavy, piled high with goods in metal and in earthenware. His owner sauntered on without noticing him otherwise than by the crack of the whip as it curled round his quivering loins. The Brabantois had paused to drink beer himself at every wayside house, but he had forbidden Patrasche to stop a moment for a draught from the canal. Going along thus, in the full sun, on a scorching highway, having eaten nothing for twenty-four hours, and, which was far worse to him, not having tasted water for near twelve, being blind with dust, sore with blows, and stupefied with the merciless weight which dragged upon his loins, Patrasche staggered and foamed a little at the mouth, and fell.

He fell in the middle of the white, dusty road, in the full glare of the sun; he was sick unto death, and motionless. His master gave him the only medicine in his pharmacy - kicks and oaths and blows with a cudgel of oak, which had been often the only food and drink, the only wage and reward, ever offered to him. But Patrasche was beyond the reach of any torture or of any curses. Patrasche lay, dead to all appearances, down in the white powder of the summer dust. After a while, finding it useless to assail his ribs with punishment and his ears with maledictions, the Brabantois - deeming life gone in him, or going, so nearly that his carcass was forever useless, unless, indeed, some one should strip it of the skin for gloves - cursed him fiercely in farewell, struck off the leathern bands of the harness, kicked his body aside into the grass, and, groaning and muttering in savage wrath, pushed the cart lazily along the road uphill, and left the dying dog for the ants to sting and for the crows to pick.

It was the last day before kermess away at Louvain, and the Brabantois was in haste to reach the fair and get a good place for his truck of brass wares. He was in fierce wrath, because Patrasche had been a strong and much-enduring animal, and because he himself had now the hard task of pushing his charette all the way to Louvain. But to stay to look after Patrasche never entered his thoughts; the beast was dying and useless, and he would steal, to replace him, the first large dog that he found wandering alone out of sight of its master. Patrasche had cost him nothing, or next to nothing, and for two long, cruel years he had made him toil ceaselessly in his service from sunrise to sunset, through summer and winter, in fair weather and foul.

He had got a fair use and a good profit out of Patrasche; being human, he was wise, and left the dog to draw his last breath alone in the ditch, and have his bloodshot eyes plucked out as they might be by the birds, whilst he himself went on his way to beg and to steal, to eat and to drink, to dance and to sing, in the mirth at Louvain. A dying dog, a dog of the cart - why should he waste hours over its agonies at peril of losing a handful of copper coins, at peril of a shout of laughter?

Patrasche lay there, flung in the grass-green ditch. It was a busy road that day, and hundreds of people, on foot and on mules, in waggons or in carts, went by, tramping quickly and joyously on to Louvain. Some saw him; most did not even look; all passed on. A dead dog more or less - it was nothing in Brabant; it would be nothing anywhere in the world.

After a time, among the holiday-makers, there came a little old man who was bent and lame, and very feeble. He was in no guise for feasting; he was very poorly and miserably clad, and he dragged his silent way slowly through the dust among the pleasure-seekers. He looked at Patrasche, paused, wondered, turned aside, then kneeled down in the rank grass and weeds of the ditch, and surveyed the dog with kindly eyes of pity. There was with him a little rosy, fair-haired, dark-eyed child of a few years old, who pattered in amid the bushes, that were for him breast-high, and stood gazing with a pretty seriousness upon the poor, great, quiet beast.

Thus it was that these two first met - the little Nello and the big Patrasche.

The upshot of that day was, that old Jehan Daas, with much laborious effort, drew the sufferer homeward to his own little hut, which was a stone's throw off amidst the fields; and there tended him with so much care that the sickness, which had been a brain seizure brought on by heat and thirst and exhaustion, with time and shade and rest passed away, and health and strength returned, and Patrasche staggered up again upon his four stout, tawny legs.

Now for many weeks he had been useless, powerless, sore, near to death; but all this time he had heard no rough word, had felt no harsh touch, but only the pitying murmurs of the child's voice and the soothing caress of the old man's hand.

In his sickness they two had grown to care for him, this lonely man and the little happy child. He had a corner of the hut, with a heap of dry grass for his bed; and they had learned to listen eagerly for his breathing in the dark night, to tell them that he lived; and when he first was well enough to essay a loud, hollow, broken bay, they laughed aloud, and almost wept together for joy at such a sign of his sure restoration; and little Nello, in delighted glee, hung round his rugged neck chains of marguerites, and kissed him with fresh and ruddy lips.

So then, when Patrasche arose, himself again, strong, big, gaunt, powerful, his great wistful eyes had a gentle astonishment in them that there were no curses to rouse him and no blows to drive him; and his heart awakened to a mighty love, which never wavered once in its fidelity while life abode with him.

But Patrasche, being a dog, was grateful. Patrasche lay pondering long with grave, tender, musing brown eyes, watching the movements of his friends.

Now, the old soldier, Jehan Daas, could do nothing for his living but limp about a little with a small cart, with which he carried daily the milk-cans of those happier neighbours who owned cattle away into the town of Antwerp. The villagers gave him the employment a little out of charity; more because it suited them well to send their milk into the town by so honest a carrier, and bide at home themselves to look after their gardens, their cows, their poultry, or their little fields. But it was becoming hard work for the old man. He was eighty-three, and Antwerp was a good league off, or more.

Patrasche watched the milk-cans come and go that one day when he had got well and was lying in the sun with the wreath of marguerites round his tawny neck.

The next morning, Patrasche, before the old man had touched the cart, arose and walked to it and placed himself betwixt its handles, and testified as plainly as dumb-show could do his desire and his ability to work in return for the bread of charity that he had eaten. Jehan Daas resisted long, for the old man was one of those who thought it a foul shame to bind dogs to labor for which Nature never formed them. But Patrasche would not be gainsaid; finding they did not harness him, he tried to draw the cart onward with his teeth.

At length Jehan Daas gave way, vanquished by the persistence and the gratitude of this creature whom he had succored. He fashioned his cart so that Patrasche could run in it, and this he did every morning of his life thenceforward.

When the winter came, Jehan Daas thanked the blessed fortune that had brought him to the dying dog in the ditch that fair-day of Louvain; for he was very old, and he grew feebler with each year, and he would ill have known how to pull his load of milk-cans over the snows and through the deep ruts in the mud if it had not been for the strength and the industry of the animal he had befriended. As for Patrasche, it seemed heaven to him. After the frightful burdens that his old master had compelled him to strain under, at the call of the whip at every step, it seemed nothing to him but amusement to step out with this little light, green cart, with its bright brass cans, by the side of the gentle old man who always paid him with a tender caress and with a kindly word. Besides, his work was over by three or four in the day, and after that time he was free to do as he would - to stretch himself, to sleep in the sun, to wander in the fields, to romp with the young child, or to play with his fellow-dogs. Patrasche was very happy.

Fortunately for his peace, his former owner was killed in a drunken brawl at the kermess of Mechlin, and so sought not after him nor disturbed him in his new and well-loved home.

A few years later, old Jehan Daas, who had always been a cripple, became so paralyzed with rheumatism that it was impossible for him to go out with the cart any more. Then little Nello, being now grown to his sixth year of age, and knowing the town well from having accompanied his grandfather so many times, took his place beside the cart, and sold the milk and received the coins in exchange, and brought them back to their respective owners with a pretty grace and seriousness which charmed all who beheld him.

The little Ardennois was a beautiful child, with dark, grave, tender eyes, and a lovely bloom upon his face, and fair locks that clustered to his throat; and many an artist sketched the group as it went by him - the green cart with the brass flagons of Teniers and Mieris and Van Tal, and the great, tawny-colored, massive dog, with his belled harness that chimed cheerily as he went, and the small figure that ran beside him which had little white feet in great wooden shoes, and a soft, grave, innocent, happy face like the little fair children of Rubens.

Nello and Patrasche did the work so well and so joyfully together that Jehan Daas himself, when the summer came and he was better again, had no need to stir out, but could sit in the doorway in the sun and see them go forth through the garden wicket, and then doze and dream and pray a little, and then awake again as the clock tolled three and watch for their return. And on their return Patrasche would shake himself free of his harness with a bay of glee, and Nello would recount with pride the doings of the day; and they would all go in together to their meal of rye bread and milk or soup, and would see the shadows lengthen over the great plain, and see the twilight veil the fair cathedral spire; and then lie down together to sleep peacefully while the old man said a prayer.

So the days and the years went on, and the lives of Nello and Patrasche were happy, innocent, and healthful.

In the spring and summer especially were they glad. Flanders is not a lovely land, and around the burg of Rubens it is perhaps least lovely of all. Corn and colza, pasture and plough, succeed each other on the characterless plain in wearying repetition, and, save by some gaunt gray tower, with its peal of pathetic bells, or some figure coming athwart the fields, made picturesque by a gleaner's bundle or a woodman's fagot, there is no change, no variety, no beauty anywhere; and he who has dwelt upon the mountains or amid the forests feels oppressed as by imprisonment with the tedium and the endlessness of that vast and dreary level. But it is green and very fertile, and it has wide horizons that have a certain charm of their own even in their dulness and monotony; and among the rushes by the waterside the flowers grow, and the trees rise tall and fresh where the barges glide, with their great hulks black against the sun, and their little green barrels and vari-coloured flags gay against the leaves. Anyway, there is greenery and breadth of space enough to be as good as beauty to a child and a dog; and these two asked no better, when their work was done, than to lie buried in the lush grasses on the side of the canal, and watch the cumbrous vessels drifting by and bringing the crisp salt smell of the sea among the blossoming scents of the country summer.

True, in the winter it was harder, and they had to rise in the darkness and the bitter cold, and they had seldom as much as they could have eaten any day; and the hut was scarce better than a shed when the nights were cold, although it looked so pretty in warm weather, buried in a great kindly clambering vine, that never bore fruit, indeed, but which covered it with luxuriant green tracery all through the months of blossom and harvest. In winter the winds found many holes in the walls of the poor little hut, and the vine was black and leafless, and the bare lands looked very bleak and drear without, and sometimes within the floor was flooded and then frozen. In winter it was hard, and the snow numbed the little white limbs of Nello, and the icicles cut the brave, untiring feet of Patrasche.

But even then they were never heard to lament, either of them. The child's wooden shoes and the dog's four legs would trot manfully together over the frozen fields to the chime of the bells on the harness; and then sometimes, in the streets of Antwerp, some housewife would bring them a bowl of soup and a handful of bread, or some kindly trader would throw some billets of fuel into the little cart as it went homeward, or some woman in their own village would bid them keep a share of the milk they carried for their own food; and they would run over the white lands, through the early darkness, bright and happy, and burst with a shout of joy into their home.

So, on the whole, it was well with them - very well; and Patrasche, meeting on the highway or in the public streets the many dogs who toiled from daybreak into nightfall, paid only with blows and curses, and loosened from the shafts with a kick to starve and freeze as best they might - Patrasche in his heart was very grateful to his fate, and thought it the fairest and the kindliest the world could hold. Though he was often very hungry indeed when he lay down at night; though he had to work in the heats of summer noons and the rasping chills of winter dawns; though his feet were often tender with wounds from the sharp edges of the jagged pavement; though he had to perform tasks beyond his strength and against his nature - yet he was grateful and content; he did his duty with each day, and the eyes that he loved smiled down on him. It was sufficient for Patrasche.

There was only one thing which caused Patrasche any uneasiness in his life, and it was this. Antwerp, as all the world knows, is full at every turn of old piles of stones, dark and ancient and majestic, standing in crooked courts, jammed against gateways and taverns, rising by the water's edge, with bells ringing above them in the air, and ever and again out of their arched doors a swell of music pealing. There they remain, the grand old sanctuaries of the past, shut in amid the squalor, the hurry, the crowds, the unloveliness, and the commerce of the modern world; and all day long the clouds drift and the birds circle and the winds sigh around them, and beneath the earth at their feet there sleeps - RUBENS.

And the greatness of the mighty master still rests upon Antwerp, and wherever we turn in its narrow streets his glory lies therein, so that all mean things are thereby transfigured; and as we pace slowly through the winding ways, and by the edge of the stagnant water, and through the noisome courts, his spirit abides with us, and the heroic beauty of his visions is about us, and the stones that once felt his footsteps and bore his shadow seem to arise and speak of him with living voices. For the city which is the tomb of Rubens still lives to us through him, and him alone.

It is so quiet there by that great white sepulchre - so quiet, save only when the organ peals and the choir cries aloud the Salve Regina or the Kyrie eleison. Sure no artist ever had a greater gravestone than that pure marble sanctuary gives to him in the heart of his birthplace in the chancel of St. Jacques.

Without Rubens, what were Antwerp? A dirty, dusky, bustling mart, which no man would ever care to look upon save the traders who do business on its wharves. With Rubens, to the whole world of men it is a sacred name, a sacred soil, a Bethlehem where a god of art saw light, a Golgotha where a god of art lies dead.

O nations! closely should you treasure your great men; for by them alone will the future know of you. Flanders in her generations has been wise. In his life she glorified this greatest of her sons, and in his death she magnifies his name. But her wisdom is very rare.

Now, the trouble of Patrasche was this. Into these great, sad piles of stones, that reared their melancholy majesty above the crowded roofs, the child Nello would many and many a time enter, and disappear through their dark, arched portals, while Patrasche, left without upon the pavement, would wearily and vainly ponder on what could be the charm which thus allured from him his inseparable and beloved companion. Once or twice he did essay to see for himself, clattering up the steps with his milk-cart behind him; but thereon he had been always sent back again summarily by a tall custodian in black clothes and silver chains of office; and fearful of bringing his little master into trouble, he desisted, and remained couched patiently before the churches until such time as the boy reappeared. It was not the fact of his going into them which disturbed Patrasche; he knew that people went to church; all the village went to the small, tumble-down, gray pile opposite the red windmill. What troubled him was that little Nello always looked strangely when he came out, always very flushed or very pale; and whenever he returned home after such visitations would sit silent and dreaming, not caring to play, but gazing out at the evening skies beyond the line of the canal, very subdued and almost sad.

What was it? wondered Patrasche. He thought it could not be good or natural for the little lad to be so grave, and in his dumb fashion he tried all he could to keep Nello by him in the sunny fields or in the busy market-place. But to the churches Nello would go; most often of all would he go to the great cathedral; and Patrasche, left without on the stones by the iron fragments of Quentin Matsys's gate, would stretch himself and yawn and sigh, and even howl now and then, all in vain, until the doors closed and the child perforce came forth again, and winding his arms about the dog's neck would kiss him on his broad, tawny-colored forehead, and murmur always the same words, "If I could only see them, Patrasche! - if I could only see them!"

What were they? pondered Patrasche, looking up with large, wistful, sympathetic eyes.

One day, when the custodian was out of the way and the doors left ajar, he got in for a moment after his little friend and saw. "They" were two great covered pictures on either side of the choir.

Nello was kneeling, rapt as in an ecstasy, before the altar-picture of the Assumption, and when he noticed Patrasche, and rose and drew the dog gently out into the air, his face was wet with tears, and he looked up at the veiled places as he passed them, and murmured to his companion, "It is so terrible not to see them, Patrasche, just because one is poor and cannot pay! He never meant that the poor should not see them when he painted them, I am sure. He would have had us see them any day, every day; that I am sure. And they keep them shrouded there - shrouded! in the dark, the beautiful things! And they never feel the light, and no eyes look on them, unless rich people come and pay. If I could only see them, I would be content to die."

But he could not see them, and Patrasche could not help him, for to gain the silver piece that the church exacts as the price for looking on the glories of the "Elevation of the Cross" and the "Descent of the Cross" was a thing as utterly beyond the powers of either of them as it would have been to scale the heights of the cathedral spire. They had never so much as a sou to spare; if they cleared enough to get a little wood for the stove, a little broth for the pot, it was the utmost they could do. And yet the heart of the child was set in sore and endless longing upon beholding the greatness of the two veiled Rubens.

The whole soul of the little Ardennois thrilled and stirred with an absorbing passion for art. Going on his ways through the old city in the early days before the sun or the people had risen, Nello, who looked only a little peasant boy, with a great dog drawing milk to sell from door to door, was in a heaven of dreams whereof Rubens was the god. Nello, cold and hungry, with stockingless feet in wooden shoes, and the winter winds blowing among his curls and lifting his poor thin garments, was in a rapture of meditation, wherein all that he saw was the beautiful fair face of the Mary of the Assumption, with the waves of her golden hair lying upon her shoulders, and the light of an eternal sun shining down upon her brow. Nello, reared in poverty, and buffeted by fortune, and untaught in letters, and unheeded by men, had the compensation or the curse which is called genius. No one knew it; he as little as any. No one knew it. Only, indeed, Patrasche, who, being with him always, saw him draw with chalk upon the stones any and every thing that grew or breathed, heard him on his little bed of hay murmur all manner of timid, pathetic prayers to the spirit of the great master; watched his gaze darken and his face radiate at the evening glow of sunset or the rosy rising of the dawn; and felt many and many a time the tears of a strange, nameless pain and joy, mingled together, fall hotly from the bright young eyes upon his own wrinkled yellow forehead.

"I should go to my grave quite content if I thought, Nello, that when thou growest a man thou couldst own this hut and the little plot of ground, and labor for thyself, and be called Baas by thy neighbours," said the old man Jehan many an hour from his bed. For to own a bit of soil, and to be called Baas (master) by the hamlet round, is to have achieved the highest ideal of a Flemish peasant; and the old soldier, who had wandered over all the earth in his youth, and had brought nothing back, deemed in his old age that to live and die on one spot in contented humility was the fairest fate he could desire for his darling. But Nello said nothing.

The same leaven was working in him that in other times begat Rubens and Jordaens and the Van Eycks, and all their wondrous tribe, and in times more recent begat in the green country of the Ardennes, where the Meuse washes the old walls of Dijon, the great artist of the Patroclus, whose genius is too near us for us aright to measure its divinity.

Nello dreamed of other things in the future than of tilling the little rood of earth, and living under the wattle roof, and being called Baas by neighbours a little poorer or a little less poor than himself. The cathedral spire, where it rose beyond the fields in the ruddy evening skies or in the dim, gray, misty mornings, said other things to him than this. But these he told only to Patrasche, whispering, childlike, his fancies in the dog's ear when they went together at their work through the fogs of the daybreak, or lay together at their rest among the rustling rushes by the water's side.

For such dreams are not easily shaped into speech to awake the slow sympathies of human auditors; and they would only have sorely perplexed and troubled the poor old man bedridden in his corner, who, for his part, whenever he had trodden the streets of Antwerp, had thought the daub of blue and red that they called a

Madonna, on the walls of the wine-shop where he drank his sou's worth of black beer, quite as good as any of the famous altarpieces for which the stranger folk traveled far and wide into Flanders from every land on which the good sun shone.

There was only one other beside Patrasche to whom Nello could talk at all of his daring fantasies. This other was little Alois, who lived at the old red mill on the grassy mound, and whose father, the miller, was the best-to-do husbandman in all the village. Little Alois was only a pretty baby with soft round, rosy features, made lovely by those sweet dark eyes that the Spanish rule has left in so many a Flemish face, in testimony of the Alvan dominion, as Spanish art has left broad-sown throughout the country majestic palaces and stately courts, gilded house-fronts and sculptured lintels - histories in blazonry and poems in stone.

Little Alois was often with Nello and Patrasche. They played in the fields, they ran in the snow, they gathered the daisies and bilberries, they went up to the old gray church together, and they often sat together by the broad wood fire in the mill-house. Little Alois, indeed, was the richest child in the hamlet. She had neither brother nor sister; her blue serge dress had never a hole in it; at kermess she had as many gilded nuts and Agni Dei in sugar as her hands could hold; and when she went up for her first communion her flaxen curls were covered with a cap of richest Mechlin lace, which had been her mother's and her grandmother's before it came to her. Men spoke already, though she had but twelve years, of the good wife she would be for their sons to woo and win; but she herself was a little gay, simple child, in no wise conscious of her heritage, and she loved no playfellows so well as Jehan Daas's grandson and his dog.

One day her father, Baas Cogez, a good man, but somewhat stern, came on a pretty group in the long meadow behind the mill, where the aftermath had that day been cut. It was his little daughter sitting amid the hay, with the great tawny head of Patrasche on her lap, and many wreaths of poppies and blue corn-flowers round them both; on a clean smooth slab of pine wood the boy Nello drew their likeness with a stick of charcoal.

The miller stood and looked at the portrait with tears in his eyes - it was so strangely like, and he loved his only child closely and well. Then he roughly chid the little girl for idling there while her mother needed her within, and sent her indoors crying and afraid; then, turning, he snatched the wood from Nello's hands. "Dost do much of such folly?" he asked, but there was a tremble in his voice.

Nello coloured and hung his head. "I draw everything I see," he murmured.

The miller was silent; then he stretched his hand out with a franc in it. "It is folly, as I say, and evil waste of time; nevertheless, it is like Alois, and will please the house-mother. Take this silver bit for it and leave it for me."

The colour died out of the face of the young Ardennois; he lifted his head and put his hands behind his back. "Keep your money and the portrait both, Baas Cogez," he said, simply. "You have been often good to me." Then he called Patrasche to him, and walked away across the fields.

"I could have seen them with that franc," he murmured to Patrasche, "but I could not sell her picture - not even for them."

Baas Cogez went into his mill-house sore troubled in his mind. "That lad must not be so much with Alois," he said to his wife that night. "Trouble may come of it hereafter; he is fifteen now, and she is twelve; and the boy is comely of face and form."

"And he is a good lad and a loyal," said the housewife, feasting her eyes on the piece of pine wood where it was throned above the chimney with a cuckoo clock in oak and a Calvary in wax.

"Yea, I do not gainsay that," said the miller, draining his pewter flagon.

"Then, if what you think of were ever to come to pass," said the wife, hesitatingly, "would it matter so much? She will have enough for both, and one cannot be better than happy."

"You are a woman, and therefore a fool," said the miller, harshly, striking his pipe on the table. "The lad is naught but a beggar, and, with these painter's fancies, worse than a beggar. Have a care that they are not together in the future, or I will send the child to the surer keeping of the nuns of the Sacred Heart."

The poor mother was terrified, and promised humbly to do his will. Not that she could bring herself altogether to separate the child from her favorite playmate, nor did the miller even desire that extreme of cruelty to a young lad who was guilty of nothing except poverty. But there were many ways in which little Alois was kept away from her chosen companion; and Nello, being a boy proud and quiet and sensitive, was quickly wounded, and ceased to turn his own steps and those of Patrasche, as he had been used to do with every moment of leisure, to the old red mill upon the slope. What his offence was he did not know; he supposed he had in some manner angered Baas Cogez by taking the portrait of Alois in the meadow; and when the child who loved him would run to him and nestle her hand in his, he would smile at her very sadly and say with a tender concern for her before himself, "Nay, Alois, do not anger your father. He thinks that I make you idle, dear, and he is not pleased that you should be with me. He is a good man and loves you well; we will not anger him, Alois."

But it was with a sad heart that he said it, and the earth did not look so bright to him as it had used to do when he went out at sunrise under the poplars down the straight roads with Patrasche. The old red mill had been a landmark to him, and he had been used to pause by it, going and coming, for a cheery greeting with its people as her little flaxen head rose above the low mill wicket, and her little rosy hands had held out a bone or a crust to Patrasche. Now the dog looked wistfully at a closed door, and the boy went on without pausing, with a pang at his heart, and the child sat within with tears dropping slowly on the knitting to which she was set on her little stool by the stove; and Baas Cogez, working among his sacks and his mill-gear, would harden his will and say to himself, "It is best so. The lad is all but a beggar, and full of idle, dreaming fooleries. Who knows what mischief might not come of it in the future?" So he was wise in his generation, and would not have the door unbarred, except upon rare and formal occasions, which seemed to have neither warmth nor mirth in them to the two children, who had been accustomed so long to a daily gleeful, careless, happy interchange of greeting, speech, and pastime, with no other watcher of their sports or auditor of their fancies than Patrasche, sagely shaking the brazen bells of his collar and responding with all a dog's swift sympathies to their every change of mood.

All this while the little panel of pine wood remained over the chimney in the mill kitchen with the cuckoo clock and the waxen Calvary; and sometimes it seemed to Nello a little hard that while his gift was accepted, he himself should be denied.

But he did not complain; it was his habit to be quiet. Old Jehan Daas had said ever to him, "We are poor; we must take what God sends - the ill with the good; the poor cannot choose."

To which the boy had always listened in silence, being reverent of his old grandfather; but nevertheless a certain vague, sweet hope, such as beguiles the children of genius, had whispered in his heart, "Yet the poor do choose sometimes - choose to be great, so that men cannot say them nay." And he thought so still in his innocence; and one day, when the little Alois, finding him by chance alone among the corn-fields by the canal, ran to him and held him close, and sobbed piteously because the morrow would be her saint's day, and for the first time in all her life her parents had failed to bid him to the little supper and romp in the great barns with which her feast-day was always celebrated, Nello had kissed her and murmured to her in firm faith, "It shall be different one day, Alois. One day that little bit of pine wood that your father has of mine shall be worth its weight in silver; and he will not shut the door against me then. Only love me always, dear little Alois; only love me always, and I will be great."

"And if I do not love you?" the pretty child asked, pouting a little through her tears, and moved by the instinctive coquetries of her sex.

Nello's eyes left her face and wandered to the distance, where, in the red and gold of the Flemish night, the cathedral spire rose. There was a smile on his face so sweet and yet so sad that little Alois was awed by it. "I will be great still," he said under his breath - "great still, or die, Alois."

"You do not love me," said the little spoiled child, pushing him away; but the boy shook his head and smiled, and went on his way through the tall yellow corn, seeing as in a vision some day in a fair future when he should come into that old familiar land and ask Alois of her people, and be not refused or denied, but received in honour; while the village folk should throng to look upon him and say in one another's ears, "Dost see him? He is a king among men; for he is a great artist and the world speaks his name; and yet he was only our poor little Nello, who was a beggar, as one may say, and only got his bread by the help of his dog." And he thought how he would fold his grandsire in furs and purples, and portray him as the old man is portrayed in the Family in the chapel of St. Jacques; and of how he would hang the throat of Patrasche with a collar of gold, and place him on his right hand, and say to the people, "This was once my only friend;" and of how he would build himself a great white marble palace, and make to himself luxuriant gardens of pleasure, on the slope looking outward to where the cathedral spire rose, and not dwell in it himself, but summon to it, as to a home, all men young and poor and friendless, but of the will to do mighty things; and of how he would say to them always, if they sought to bless his name, "Nay, do not thank me - thank Rubens. Without him, what should I have been?" And these dreams - beautiful, impossible, innocent, free of all selfishness, full of heroical worship - were so closely about him as he went that he was happy - happy even on this sad anniversary of Alois's saint's day, when he and Patrasche went home by themselves to the little dark hut and the meal of black bread, while in the mill-house all the children of the village sang and laughed, and ate the big round cakes of Dijon and the almond gingerbread of Brabant, and danced in the great barn to the light of the stars and the music of flute and fiddle.

"Never mind, Patrasche," he said, with his arms round the dog's neck, as they both sat in the door of the hut, where the sounds of the mirth at the mill came down to them on the night air; "never mind. It shall all be changed by-and-by."

He believed in the future; Patrasche, of more experience and of more philosophy, thought that the loss of the mill supper in the present was ill compensated by dreams of milk and honey in some vague hereafter. And Patrasche growled whenever he passed by Baas Cogez.

"This is Alois's name-day, is it not?" said the old man Daas that night, from the corner where he was stretched upon his bed of sacking.

The boy gave a gesture of assent; he wished that the old man's memory had erred a little, instead of keeping such sure account.

"And why not there?" his grandfather pursued. "Thou hast never missed a year before, Nello."

"Thou art too sick to leave," murmured the lad, bending his handsome head over the bed.

"Tut! tut! Mother Nulette would have come and sat with me, as she does scores of times. What is the cause, Nello?" the old man persisted. "Thou surely hast not had ill words with the little one?"

"Nay, grandfather, never," said the boy quickly, with a hot colour in his bent face. "Simply and truly, Baas Cogez did not have me asked this year. He has taken some whim against me."

"But thou hast done nothing wrong?"

"That I know - nothing. I took the portrait of Alois on a piece of pine; that is all."

"Ah!" The old man was silent; the truth suggested itself to him with the boy's innocent answer. He was tied to a bed of dried leaves in the corner of a wattle hut, but he had not wholly forgotten what the ways of the world were like.

He drew Nello's fair head fondly to his breast with a tenderer gesture. "Thou art very poor, my child," he said, with a quiver the more in his aged, trembling voice; "so poor! It is very hard for thee."

"Nay, I am rich," murmured Nello; and in his innocence he thought so; rich with the imperishable powers that are mightier than the might of kings. And he went and stood by the door of the hut in the quiet autumn night, and watched the stars troop by and the tall poplars bend and shiver in the wind. All the casements of the mill-house were lighted, and every now and then the notes of the flute came to him. The tears fell down his cheeks, for he was but a child; yet he smiled, for he said to himself, "In the future!" He stayed there until all was quite still and dark; then he and Patrasche went within and slept together, long and deeply, side by side.

Now he had a secret which only Patrasche knew. There was a little outhouse to the hut which no one entered but himself - a dreary place, but with abundant clear light from the north. Here he had fashioned himself rudely an easel in rough lumber, and here, on a great gray sea of stretched paper, he had given shape to one of the innumerable fancies which possessed his brain. No one had ever taught him anything; colours he had no means to buy; he had gone without bread many a time to procure even the few rude vehicles that he had here; and it was only in black or white that he could fashion the things he saw. This great figure which he had drawn here in chalk was only an old man sitting on a fallen tree - only that. He had seen old Michel, the woodman, sitting so at evening many a time. He had never had a soul to tell him of outline or perspective, of anatomy or of shadow; and yet he had given all the weary, worn-out age, all the sad, quiet patience, all the rugged, care-worn pathos of his original, and given them so that the old, lonely figure was a poem, sitting there meditative and alone, on the dead tree, with the darkness of the descending night behind him.

It was rude, of course, in a way, and had many faults, no doubt; and yet it was real, true in nature, true in art, and very mournful, and in a manner beautiful.

Patrasche had lain quiet countless hours watching its gradual creation after the labor of each day was done, and he knew that Nello had a hope - vain and wild perhaps, but strongly cherished - of sending this great drawing to compete for a prize of two hundred francs a year which it was announced in Antwerp would be open to every lad of talent, scholar or peasant, under eighteen, who would attempt to win it with some unaided work of chalk or pencil. Three of the foremost artists in the town of Rubens were to be the judges and elect the victor according to his merits.

All the spring and summer and autumn Nello had been at work upon this treasure, which if triumphant, would build him his first step toward independence and the mysteries of the art which he blindly, ignorantly, and yet passionately adored.

He said nothing to any one; his grandfather would not have understood, and little Alois was lost to him. Only to Patrasche he told all, and whispered, "Rubens would give it me, I think, if he knew."

Patrasche thought so too, for he knew that Rubens had loved dogs or he had never painted them with such exquisite fidelity; and men who loved dogs were, as Patrasche knew, always pitiful.

The drawings were to go in on the first day of December, and the decision be given on the twenty-fourth, so that he who should win might rejoice with all his people at the Christmas season.

In the twilight of a bitter wintry day, and with a beating heart, now quick with hope, now faint with fear, Nello placed the great picture on his little green milk-cart, and took it, with the help of Patrasche, into the town, and there left it, as enjoined, at the doors of a public building.

"Perhaps it is worth nothing at all. How can I tell?" he thought, with the heart-sickness of a great timidity. Now that he had left it there, it seemed to him so hazardous, so vain, so foolish, to dream that he, a little lad with bare feet who barely knew his letters, could do anything at which great painters, real artists, could ever deign to look. Yet he took heart as he went by the cathedral; the lordly form of Rubens seemed to rise from the fog and the darkness, and to loom in its magnificence before him, while the lips, with their kindly smile, seemed to him to murmur, "Nay, have courage! It was not by a weak heart and by faint fears that I wrote my name for all time upon Antwerp."

Nello ran home through the cold night, comforted. He had done his best; the rest must be as God willed, he thought, in that innocent, unquestioning faith which had been taught him in the little gray chapel among the willows and the poplar-trees.

The winter was very sharp already. That night, after they reached the hut, snow fell, and fell for very many days after that; so that the paths and the divisions in the fields were all obliterated, and all the smaller streams were frozen over, and the cold was intense upon the plains. Then, indeed, it became hard work to go round for the milk while the world was all dark, and carry it through the darkness to the silent town. Hard work, especially for Patrasche, for the passage of the years that were only bringing Nello a stronger youth were bringing him old age, and his joints were stiff and his bones ached often. But he would never give up his share of the labour. Nello would fain have spared him and drawn the cart himself, but Patrasche would not allow it. All he would ever permit or accept was the help of a thrust from behind to the truck as it lumbered along through the ice-ruts. Patrasche had lived in harness, and he was proud of it. He suffered a great deal sometimes from frost and the terrible roads and the rheumatic pains of his limbs; but he only drew his breath hard and bent his stout neck, and trod onward with steady patience.

"Rest thee at home, Patrasche; it is time thou didst rest, and I can quite well push in the cart by myself," urged Nello many a morning; but Patrasche, who understood him aright, would no more have consented to stay at home than a veteran soldier to shirk when the charge was sounding; and every day he would rise and place himself in his shafts, and plod along over the snow through the fields that his four round feet had left their print upon so many, many years.

"One must never rest till one dies," thought Patrasche; and sometimes it seemed to him that that time of rest for him was not very far off. His sight was less clear than it had been, and it gave him pain to rise after the night's sleep, though he would never lie a moment in his straw when once the bell of the chapel tolling five let him know that the daybreak of labor had begun.

"My poor Patrasche, we shall soon lie quiet together, you and I," said old Jehan Daas, stretching out to stroke the head of Patrasche with the old withered hand which had always shared with him its one poor crust of bread; and the hearts of the old man and the old dog ached together with one thought: When they were gone who would care for their darling?

One afternoon, as they came back from Antwerp over the snow, which had become hard and smooth as marble over all the Flemish plains, they found dropped in the road a pretty little puppet, a tambourine player, all scarlet and gold, about six inches high, and, unlike greater personages when Fortune lets them drop, quite unspoiled and unhurt by its fall. It was a pretty toy. Nello tried to find its owner, and, failing, thought that it was just the thing to please Alois.

It was quite night when he passed the mill-house; he knew the little window of her room; it could be no harm, he thought, if he gave her his little piece of treasure-trove - they had been play-fellows so long. There was a shed with a sloping roof beneath her casement; he climbed it and tapped softly at the lattice; there was a little light within. The child opened it and looked out half frightened.

Nello put the tambourine player into her hands. "Here is a doll I found in the snow, Alois. Take it," he whispered; "take it, and God bless thee, dear!"

He slid down from the shed roof before she had time to thank him, and ran off through the darkness.

That night there was a fire at the mill. Out-buildings and much corn were destroyed, although the mill itself and the dwelling-house were unharmed. All the village was out in terror, and engines came tearing through the snow from Antwerp. The miller was insured, and would lose nothing; nevertheless, he was in furious wrath, and declared aloud that the fire was due to no accident, but to some foul intent.

Nello, awakened from his sleep, ran to help with the rest. Baas Cogez thrust him angrily aside. "Thou wert loitering here after dark," he said roughly. "I believe, on my soul, that thou dost know more of the fire than any one."

Nello heard him in silence, stupefied, not supposing that any one could say such things except in jest, and not comprehending how any one could pass a jest at such a time.

Nevertheless, the miller said the brutal thing openly to many of his neighbours in the day that followed; and though no serious charge was ever preferred against the lad, it got bruited about that Nello had been seen in the mill-yard after dark on some unspoken errand, and that he bore Baas Cogez a grudge for forbidding his intercourse with little Alois; and so the hamlet, which followed the sayings of its richest landowner servilely, and whose families all hoped to secure the riches of Alois in some future time for their sons, took the hint to give grave looks and cold words to old Jehan Daas's grandson. No one said anything to him openly, but all the village agreed together to humour the miller's prejudice, and at the cottages and farms where Nello and Patrasche called every morning for the milk for Antwerp, downcast glances and brief phrases replaced to them the broad smiles and cheerful greetings to which they had been always used. No one really credited the miller's absurd suspicions, nor the outrageous accusations born of them; but the people were all very poor and very ignorant, and the one rich man of the place had pronounced against him. Nello, in his innocence and his friendlessness, had no strength to stem the popular tide.

"Thou art very cruel to the lad," the miller's wife dared to say, weeping, to her lord. "Sure, he is an innocent lad and a faithful, and would never dream of any such wickedness, however sore his heart might be."

But Baas Cogez being an obstinate man, having once said a thing, held to it doggedly, though in his innermost soul he knew well the injustice that he was committing.

Meanwhile, Nello endured the injury done against him with a certain proud patience that disdained to complain; he only gave way a little when he was quite alone with old Patrasche. Besides, he thought, "If it should win! They will be sorry then, perhaps."

Still, to a boy not quite sixteen, and who had dwelt in one little world all his short life, and in his childhood had been caressed and applauded on all sides, it was a hard trial to have the whole of that little world turn against him for naught. Especially hard in that bleak, snow-bound, famine-stricken winter-time, when the only light and warmth there could be found abode beside the village hearths and in the kindly greetings of neighbours. In the winter-time all drew nearer to each other, all to all, except to Nello and Patrasche, with whom none now would have anything to do, and who were left to fare as they might with the old paralyzed, bedridden man in the little cabin, whose fire was often low, and whose board was often without bread; for there was a buyer from Antwerp who had taken to drive his mule in of a day for the milk of the various dairies, and there were only three or four of the people who had refused his terms of purchase and remained faithful to the little green cart. So that the burden which Patrasche drew had become very light, and the centime pieces in Nello's pouch had become, alas! very small likewise.

The dog would stop, as usual, at all the familiar gates which were now closed to him, and look up at them with wistful, mute appeal; and it cost the neighbours a pang to shut their doors and their hearts, and let Patrasche draw his cart on again, empty. Nevertheless, they did it, for they desired to please Baas Cogez.

Noel was close at hand.

The weather was very wild and cold; the snow was six feet deep, and the ice was firm enough to bear oxen and men upon it everywhere. At this season the little village was always gay and cheerful. At the poorest dwelling there were possets and cakes, joking and dancing, sugared saints and gilded Jesus. The merry Flemish bells jingled everywhere on the horses; everywhere within doors some well-filled soup-pot sang and smoked over the stove; and everywhere over the snow without laughing maidens pattered in bright kerchiefs and stout kirtles, going to and from the mass. Only in the little hut it was very dark and very cold.

Nello and Patrasche were left utterly alone, for one night in the week before the Christmas Day, death entered there, and took away from life forever old Jehan Daas, who had never known life aught save its poverty and its pains. He had long been half dead, incapable of any movement except a feeble gesture, and powerless for anything beyond a gentle word; and yet his loss fell on them both with a great horror in it;

they mourned him passionately. He had passed away from them in his sleep, and when in the gray dawn they learned their bereavement, unutterable solitude and desolation seemed to close around them. He had long been only a poor, feeble, paralyzed old man, who could not raise a hand in their defence; but he had loved them well, his smile had always welcomed their return. They mourned for him unceasingly, refusing to be comforted, as in the white winter day they followed the deal shell that held his body to the nameless grave by the little gray church. They were his only mourners, these two whom he had left friendless upon earth - the young boy and the old dog.

"Surely, he will relent now and let the poor lad come hither?" thought the miller's wife, glancing at her husband where he smoked by the hearth.

Baas Cogez knew her thought, but he hardened his heart, and would not unbar his door as the little, humble funeral went by. "The boy is a beggar," he said to himself; "he shall not be about Alois."

The woman dared not say anything aloud, but when the grave was closed and the mourners had gone, she put a wreath of immortelles into Alois's hands and bade her go and lay it reverently on the dark, unmarked mound where the snow was displaced.

Nello and Patrasche went home with broken hearts. But even of that poor, melancholy, cheerless home they were denied the consolation. There was a month's rent overdue for their little home, and when Nello had paid the last sad service to the dead he had not a coin left. He went and begged grace of the owner of the hut, a cobbler who went every Sunday night to drink his pint of wine and smoke with Baas Cogez. The cobbler would grant no mercy. He was a harsh, miserly man, and loved money. He claimed in default of his rent every stick and stone, every pot and pan, in the hut, and bade Nello and Patrasche be out of it on the morrow.

Now, the cabin was lowly enough, and in some sense miserable enough, and yet their hearts clove to it with a great affection. They had been so happy there, and in the summer, with its clambering vine and its flowering beans, it was so pretty and bright in the midst of the sun-lighted fields! Their life in it had been full of labor and privation, and yet they had been so well content, so gay of heart, running together to meet the old man's never-failing smile of welcome!

All night long the boy and the dog sat by the fireless hearth in the darkness, drawn close together for warmth and sorrow. Their bodies were insensible to the cold, but their hearts seemed frozen in them.

When the morning broke over the white, chill earth it was the morning of Christmas Eve. With a shudder, Nello clasped close to him his only friend, while his tears fell hot and fast on the dog's frank forehead. "Let us go, Patrasche - dear, dear Patrasche," he murmured. "We will not wait to be kicked out; let us go."

Patrasche had no will but his, and they went sadly, side by side, out from the little place which was so dear to them both, and in which every humble, homely thing was to them precious and beloved. Patrasche drooped his head wearily as he passed by his own green cart; it was no longer his, - it had to go with the rest to pay the rent, - and his brass harness lay idle and glittering on the snow. The dog could have lain down beside it and died for very heart-sickness as he went, but while the lad lived and needed him Patrasche would not yield and give way.

They took the old accustomed road into Antwerp. The day had yet scarce more than dawned; most of the shutters were still closed, but some of the villagers were about. They took no notice while the dog and the boy passed by them. At one door Nello paused and looked wistfully within; his grandfather had done many a kindly turn in neighbour's service to the people who dwelt there.

"Would you give Patrasche a crust?" he said, timidly. "He is old, and he has had nothing since last forenoon."

The woman shut the door hastily, murmuring some vague saying about wheat and rye being very dear that season. The boy and the dog went on again wearily; they asked no more.

By slow and painful ways they reached Antwerp as the chimes tolled ten.

"If I had anything about me I could sell to get him bread!" thought Nello; but he had nothing except the wisp of linen and serge that covered him, and his pair of wooden shoes.

Patrasche understood, and nestled his nose into the lad's hand as though to pray him not to be disquieted for any woe or want of his.

The winner of the drawing prize was to be proclaimed

at noon, and to the public building where he had left his treasure Nello made his way. On the steps and in the entrance-hall there was a crowd of youths, - some of his age, some older, all with parents or relatives or friends. His heart was sick with fear as he went among them holding Patrasche close to him. The great bells of the city clashed out the hour of noon with brazen clamour. The doors of the inner hall were opened; the eager, panting throng rushed in. It was known that the selected picture would be raised above the rest upon a wooden dais.

A mist obscured Nello's sight, his head swam, his limbs almost failed him. When his vision cleared he saw the drawing raised on high; it was not his own! A slow, sonorous voice was proclaiming aloud that victory had been adjudged to Stephen Kiesslinger, born in the burg of Antwerp, son of a wharfinger in that town.

When Nello recovered his consciousness he was lying on the stones without, and Patrasche was trying with every art he knew to call him back to life. In the distance a throng of the youths of Antwerp were shouting around their successful comrade, and escorting him with acclamations to his home upon the quay.

The boy staggered to his feet and drew the dog into his embrace. "It is all over, dear Patrasche," he murmured - "all over!"

He rallied himself as best he could, for he was weak from fasting, and retraced his steps to the village. Patrasche paced by his side with his head drooping and his old limbs feeble from hunger and sorrow.

The snow was falling fast; a keen hurricane blew from the north; it was bitter as death on the plains. It took them long to traverse the familiar path, and the bells were sounding four of the clock as they approached the hamlet. Suddenly Patrasche paused, arrested by a scent in the snow, scratched, whined, and drew out with his teeth a small case of brown leather. He held it up to Nello in the darkness. Where they were there stood a little Calvary, and a lamp burned dully under the cross; the boy mechanically turned the case to the light; on it was the name of Baas Cogez, and within it were notes for two thousand francs.

The sight roused the lad a little from his stupor. He thrust it in his shirt, and stroked Patrasche and drew him onward. The dog looked up wistfully in his face.

Nello made straight for the mill-house, and went to the house door and struck on its panels. The miller's wife opened it weeping, with little Alois clinging close to her skirts. "Is it thee, thou poor lad?" she said kindly, through her tears. "Get thee gone ere the Baas see thee. We are in sore trouble to-night. He is out seeking for a power of money that he has let fall riding homeward, and in this snow he never will find it; and God knows it will go nigh to ruin us. It is Heaven's own judgment for the things we have done to thee."

Nello put the note-case in her hand and called Patrasche within the house. "Patrasche found the money to-night," he said quickly. "Tell Baas Cogez so; I think he will not deny the dog shelter and food in his old age. Keep him from pursuing me, and I pray of you to be good to him."

Ere either woman or dog knew what he meant he had

stooped and kissed Patrasche, then closed the door hurriedly, and disappeared in the gloom of the fast-falling night.

The woman and the child stood speechless with joy and fear; Patrasche vainly spent the fury of his anguish against the iron-bound oak of the barred house door. They did not dare unbar the door and let him forth; they tried all they could to solace him. They brought him sweet cakes and juicy meats; they tempted him with the best they had; they tried to lure him to abide by the warmth of the hearth; but it was of no avail. Patrasche refused to be comforted or to stir from the barred portal.

It was six o'clock when from an opposite entrance the miller at last came, jaded and broken, into his wife's presence. "It is lost forever," he said, with an ashen cheek and a quiver in his stern voice. "We have looked with lanterns everywhere; it is gone - the little maiden's portion and all!"

His wife put the money into his hand, and told him how it had come to her. The strong man sank trembling into a seat and covered his face, ashamed and almost afraid. "I have been cruel to the lad," he muttered at length; "I deserved not to have good at his hands."

Little Alois, taking courage, crept close to her father and nestled against him her fair curly head. "Nello may come here again, father?" she whispered. "He may come to-morrow as he used to do?"

The miller pressed her in his arms; his hard, sunburnt face was very pale and his mouth trembled. "Surely, surely," he answered his child. "He shall bide here on

Christmas Day, and any other day he will. God helping me, I will make amends to the boy - I will make amends."

Little Alois kissed him in gratitude and joy; then slid from his knees and ran to where the dog kept watch by the door. "And to-night I may feast Patrasche?" she cried in a child's thoughtless glee.

Her father bent his head gravely: "Ay, ay! let the dog have the best;" for the stern old man was moved and shaken to his heart's depths.

It was Christmas eve, and the mill-house was filled with oak logs and squares of turf, with cream and honey, with meat and bread, and the rafters were hung with wreaths of evergreen, and the Calvary and the cuckoo clock looked out from a mass of holly. There were little paper lanterns, too, for Alois, and toys of various fashions and sweetmeats in bright-pictured papers. There were light and warmth and abundance everywhere, and the child would fain have made the dog a guest honoured and feasted.

But Patrasche would neither lie in the warmth nor share in the cheer. Famished he was and very cold, but without Nello he would partake neither of comfort nor food. Against all temptation he was proof, and close against the door he leaned always, watching only for a means of escape.

"He wants the lad," said Baas Cogez. "Good dog! good dog! I will go over to the lad the first thing at day-dawn." For no one but Patrasche knew that Nello had left the hut, and no one but Patrasche divined that Nello had gone to face starvation and misery alone.

The mill kitchen was very warm; great logs crackled and flamed on the hearth; neighbours came in for a glass of wine and a slice of the fat goose baking for supper. Alois, gleeful and sure of her playmate back on the morrow, bounded and sang and tossed back her yellow hair. Baas Cogez, in the fulness of his heart, smiled on her through moistened eyes, and spoke of the way in which he would befriend her favourite companion; the house-mother sat with calm, contented face at the spinning-wheel; the cuckoo in the clock chirped mirthful hours. Amidst it all Patrasche was bidden with a thousand words of welcome to tarry there a cherished guest. But neither peace nor plenty could allure him where Nello was not.

When the supper smoked on the board, and the voices were loudest and gladdest, and the Christ-child brought choicest gifts to Alois, Patrasche, watching always an occasion, glided out when the door was unlatched by a careless new-comer, and, as swiftly as his weak and tired limbs would bear him sped over the snow in the bitter, black night. He had only one thought - to follow Nello. A human friend might have paused for the pleasant meal, the cheery warmth, the cosey slumber; but that was not the friendship of Patrasche. He remembered a bygone time, when an old man and a little child had found him sick unto death in the wayside ditch.

Snow had fallen freshly all the evening long; it was now nearly ten; the trail of the boy's footsteps was almost obliterated. It took Patrasche long to discover any scent. When at last he found it, it was lost again quickly, and lost and recovered, and again lost and again recovered, a hundred times or more.

The night was very wild. The lamps under the wayside crosses were blown out; the roads were sheets of ice; the impenetrable darkness hid every trace of habitations; there was no living thing abroad. All the cattle were housed, and in all the huts and homesteads men and women rejoiced and feasted. There was only Patrasche out in the cruel cold - old and famished and full of pain, but with the strength and the patience of a great love to sustain him in his search.

The trail of Nello's steps, faint and obscure as it was under the new snow, went straightly along the accustomed tracks into Antwerp. It was past midnight when Patrasche traced it over the boundaries of the town and into the narrow, tortuous, gloomy streets. It was all quite dark in the town, save where some light gleamed ruddily through the crevices of house shutters, or some group went homeward with lanterns chanting drinking-songs. The streets were all white with ice; the high walls and roofs loomed black against them. There was scarce a sound save the riot of the winds down the passages as they tossed the creaking signs and shook the tall lamp-irons.

So many passers-by had trodden through and through the snow, so many diverse paths had crossed and recrossed each other, that the dog had a hard task to retain any hold on the track he followed. But he kept on his way, though the cold pierced him to the bone, and the jagged ice cut his feet, and the hunger in his body gnawed like a rat's teeth. He kept on his way, - a poor gaunt, shivering thing, - and by long patience traced the steps he loved into the very heart of the burg and up to the steps of the great cathedral.

"He is gone to the things that he loved," thought

Patrasche; he could not understand, but he was full of sorrow and of pity for the art passion that to him was so incomprehensible and yet so sacred.

The portals of the cathedral were unclosed after the midnight mass. Some heedlessness in the custodians, too eager to go home and feast or sleep, or too drowsy to know whether they turned the keys aright, had left one of the doors unlocked. By that accident the footfalls Patrasche sought had passed through into the building, leaving the white marks of snow upon the dark stone floor. By that slender white thread, frozen as it fell, he was guided through the intense silence, through the immensity of the vaulted space - guided straight to the gates of the chancel, and, stretched there upon the stones, he found Nello. He crept up, and touched the face of the boy. "Didst thou dream that I should be faithless and forsake thee? I - a dog?" said that mute caress.

The lad raised himself with a low cry and clasped him close. "Let us lie down and die together," he murmured. "Men have no need of us, and we are all alone."

In answer, Patrasche crept closer yet, and laid his head upon the young boy's breast. The great tears stood in his brown, sad eyes; not for himself - for himself he was happy.

They lay close together in the piercing cold. The blasts that blew over the Flemish dikes from the northern seas were like waves of ice, which froze every living thing they touched. The interior of the immense vault of stone in which they were was even more bitterly chill than the snow-covered plains without. Now and then a bat moved in the shadows; now and then a gleam of light came on the ranks of carven figures. Under the Rubens they lay together quite still, and soothed almost into a dreaming slumber by the numbing narcotic of the cold. Together they dreamed of the old glad days when they had chased each other through the flowering grasses of the summer meadows, or sat hidden in the tall bulrushes by the water's side, watching the boats go seaward in the sun.

Suddenly through the darkness a great white radiance streamed through the vastness of the aisles; the moon, that was at her height, had broken through the clouds; the snow had ceased to fall; the light reflected from the snow without was clear as the light of dawn. It fell through the arches full upon the two pictures above, from which the boy on his entrance had flung back the veil: the "Elevation" and the "Descent of the Cross" were for one instant visible.

Nello rose to his feet and stretched his arms to them; the tears of a passionate ecstasy glistened on the paleness of his face. "I have seen them at last!" he cried aloud. "O God, it is enough!"

His limbs failed under him, and he sank upon his knees, still gazing upward at the majesty that he adored. For a few brief moments the light illumined the divine visions that had been denied to him so long - light clear and sweet and strong as though it streamed from the throne of Heaven. Then suddenly it passed away; once more a great darkness covered the face of Christ.

The arms of the boy drew close again the body of the dog. "We shall see His face - there," he murmured;

"and He will not part us, I think."

On the morrow, by the chancel of the cathedral, the people of Antwerp found them both. They were both dead; the cold of the night had frozen into stillness alike the young life and the old. When the Christmas morning broke and the priests came to the temple, they saw them lying thus on the stones together. Above, the veils were drawn back from the great visions of Rubens, and the fresh rays of the sunrise touched the thorn-crowned head of the Christ.

As the day grew on there came an old, hard-featured man who wept as women weep. "I was cruel to the lad," he muttered; "and now I would have made amends, - yea, to the half of my substance, - and he should have been to me as a son."

There came also, as the day grew apace, a painter who had fame in the world, and who was liberal of hand and of spirit. "I seek one who should have had the prize yesterday had worth won," he said to the people - "a boy of rare promise and genius. An old wood-cutter on a fallen tree at eventide - that was all his theme; but there was greatness for the future in it. I would fain find him, and take him with me and teach him art."

And a little child with curling fair hair, sobbing bitterly as she clung to her father's arm, cried aloud, "Oh, Nello, come! We have all ready for thee. The Christ-child's hands are full of gifts, and the old piper will play for us; and the mother says thou shalt stay by the hearth and burn nuts with us all the Noel week long - yes, even to the Feast of the Kings! And Patrasche will be so happy! Oh, Nello, wake and come!"

But the young pale face, turned upward to the light of the great Rubens with a smile upon its mouth, answered them all, "It is too late."

For the sweet, sonorous bells went ringing through the frost, and the sunlight shone upon the plains of snow, and the populace trooped gay and glad through the streets, but Nello and Patrasche no more asked charity at their hands. All they needed now Antwerp gave unbidden.

Death had been more pitiful to them than longer life would have been. It had taken the one in the loyalty of love, and the other in the innocence of faith, from a world which for love has no recompense and for faith no fulfilment.

All their lives they had been together, and in their deaths they were not divided; for when they were found the arms of the boy were folded too closely around the dog to be severed without violence, and the people of their little village, contrite and ashamed, implored a special grace for them, and, making them one grave, laid them to rest there side by side - forever!

## MARKHEIM

"Yes," said the dealer, "our windfalls are of various kinds. Some customers are ignorant, and then I touch a dividend on my superior knowledge. Some are dishonest," and here he held up the candle, so that the light fell strongly on his visitor, "and in that case," he continued, "I profit by my virtue."

Markheim had but just entered from the daylight streets, and his eyes had not yet grown familiar with the mingled shine and darkness in the shop. At these pointed words, and before the near presence of the flame, he blinked painfully and looked aside.

The dealer chuckled. "You come to me on Christmas Day," he resumed, "when you know that I am alone in my house, put up my shutters, and make a point of refusing business. Well, you will have to pay for that; you will have to pay for my loss of time, when I should be balancing my books; you will have to pay, besides, for a kind of manner that I remark in you to-day very strongly. I am the essence of discretion, and ask no awkward questions; but when a customer cannot look me in the eye, he has to pay for it." The dealer once more chuckled; and then, changing to his usual business voice, though still with a note of irony, "You can give, as usual, a clear account of how you came into the possession of the object?" he continued. "Still your uncle's cabinet? A remarkable collector, sir!"

And the little pale, round-shouldered dealer stood almost on tip-toe, looking over the top of his gold spectacles, and nodding his head with every mark of disbelief. Markheim returned his gaze with one of infinite pity, and a touch of horror.

"This time," said he, "you are in error. I have not come to sell, but to buy. I have no curios to dispose of; my uncle's cabinet is bare to the wainscot; even were it still intact, I have done well on the Stock Exchange, and should more likely add to it than otherwise, and my errand to-day is simplicity itself. I seek a Christmas present for a lady," he continued, waxing more fluent as he struck into the speech he had prepared; "and certainly I owe you every excuse for thus disturbing you upon so small a matter. But the thing was neglected yesterday; I must produce my little compliment at dinner; and, as you very well know, a rich marriage is not a thing to be neglected."

There followed a pause, during which the dealer seemed to weigh this statement incredulously. The ticking of many clocks among the curious lumber of the shop, and the faint rushing of the cabs in a near thoroughfare, filled up the interval of silence.

"Well, sir," said the dealer, "be it so. You are an old customer after all; and if, as you say, you have the chance of a good marriage, far be it from me to be an obstacle. Here is a nice thing for a lady now," he went on, "this hand-glass - fifteenth century, warranted; comes from a good collection, too; but I reserve the name, in the interests of my customer, who was just like yourself, my dear sir, the nephew and sole heir of a remarkable collector."

The dealer, while he thus ran on in his dry and biting voice, had stooped to take the object from its place; and, as he had done so, a shock had passed through Markheim, a start both of hand and foot, a sudden leap of many tumultuous passions to the face. It passed as swiftly as it came, and left no trace beyond a certain trembling of the hand that now received the glass.

"A glass," he said hoarsely, and then paused, and repeated it more clearly. "A glass? For Christmas? Surely not?"

"And why not?" cried the dealer. "Why not a glass?"

Markheim was looking upon him with an indefinable expression. "You ask me why not?" he said. "Why, look here - look in it - look at yourself! Do you like to see it? No! nor I - nor any man."

The little man had jumped back when Markheim had so suddenly confronted him with the mirror; but now, perceiving there was nothing worse on hand, he chuckled. "Your future lady, sir, must be pretty hard favoured," said he.

"I ask you," said Markheim, "for a Christmas present, and you give me this - this damned reminder of years, and sins and follies - this hand-conscience! Did you mean it? Had you a thought in your mind? Tell me. It will be better for you if you do. Come, tell me about yourself. I hazard a guess now, that you are in secret a very charitable man."

The dealer looked closely at his companion. It was very odd, Markheim did not appear to be laughing; there was something in his face like an eager sparkle of hope, but nothing of mirth.

"What are you driving at?" the dealer asked.

"Not charitable?" returned the other, gloomily. "Not charitable; not pious; not scrupulous; unloving, unbeloved; a hand to get money, a safe to keep it. Is that all? Dear God, man, is that all?"

"I will tell you what it is," began the dealer, with some sharpness, and then broke off again into a chuckle. "But I see this is a love match of yours, and you have been drinking the lady's health."

"Ah!" cried Markheim, with a strange curiosity. "Ah, have you been in love? Tell me about that."

"I," cried the dealer. "I in love! I never had the time, nor have I the time to-day for all this nonsense. Will you take the glass?"

"Where is the hurry?" returned Markheim. "It is very pleasant to stand here talking; and life is so short and insecure that I would not hurry away from any pleasure - no, not even from so mild a one as this. We should rather cling, cling to what little we can get, like a man at a cliff's edge. Every second is a cliff, if you think upon it - a cliff a mile high - high enough, if we fall, to dash us out of every feature of humanity. Hence it is best to talk pleasantly. Let us talk of each other; why should we wear this mask? Let us be confidential. Who knows? we might become friends."

"I have just one word to say to you," said the dealer. "Either make your purchase, or walk out of my shop."

"True, true," said Markheim. "Enough fooling. To business. Show me something else."

The dealer stooped once more, this time to replace the glass upon the shelf, his thin blond hair falling over his eyes as he did so. Markheim moved a little nearer, with one hand in the pocket of his greatcoat; he drew himself up and filled his lungs; at the same time many different emotions were depicted together on his face - terror, horror, and resolve, fascination and a physical repulsion; and through a haggard lift of his upper lip, his teeth looked out.

"This, perhaps, may suit," observed the dealer. And then, as he began to rearise, Markheim bounded from behind upon his victim. The long, skewer-like dagger flashed and fell. The dealer struggled like a hen, striking his temple on the shelf, and then tumbled on the floor in a heap.

Time had some score of small voices in that shop - some stately and slow as was becoming to their great age; others garrulous and hurried. All these told out the seconds in an intricate chorus of tickings. Then the passage of a lad's feet, heavily running on the pavement, broke in upon these smaller voices and startled Markheim into the consciousness of his surroundings. He looked about him awfully. The candle stood on the counter, its flame solemnly wagging in a draught; and by that inconsiderable movement the whole room was filled with noiseless bustle and kept heaving like a sea: the tall shadows nodding, the gross blots of darkness swelling and dwindling as with respiration, the faces of the portraits and the china gods changing and wavering like images in water. The inner door stood ajar, and peered into that leaguer of shadows with a long slit of daylight like a pointing finger.

From these fear-stricken rovings, Markheim's eyes returned to the body of his victim, where it lay, both humped and sprawling, incredibly small and strangely meaner than in life. In these poor, miserly clothes, in that ungainly attitude, the dealer lay like so much sawdust. Markheim had feared to see it, and, lo! it was nothing. And yet, as he gazed, this bundle of old clothes and pool of blood began to find eloquent voices. There it must lie; there was none to work the cunning hinges or direct the miracle of locomotion; there it must lie till it was found. Found! ay, and then? Then would this dead flesh lift up a cry that would ring over England, and fill the world with the echoes of pursuit. Ay, dead or not, this was still the enemy. "Time was that when the brains were out," he thought; and the first word struck into his mind. Time, now that the deed was accomplished - time, which had closed for the victim, had become instant and momentous for the slayer.

The thought was yet in his mind, when, first one and then another, with every variety of pace and voice - one deep as the bell from a cathedral turret, another ringing on its treble notes the prelude of a waltz, - the clocks began to strike the hour of three in the afternoon.

The sudden outbreak of so many tongues in that dumb chamber staggered him. He began to bestir himself, going to and fro with the candle, beleaguered by moving shadows, and startled to the soul by chance reflections. In many rich mirrors, some of home design, some from Venice or Amsterdam, he saw his face repeated and repeated, as it were an army of spies; his own eyes met and detected him; and the sound of his own steps, lightly as they fell, vexed the surrounding quiet. And still, as he continued to fill his pockets, his mind accused him with a sickening iteration, of the thousand faults of his design. He should have chosen a more quiet hour; he should have prepared an alibi; he should not have used a knife; he should have been more cautious, and only bound and gagged the dealer, and not killed him; he should have been more bold, and killed the servant also; he should have done all things otherwise. Poignant regrets, weary, incessant toiling of the mind to change what was unchangeable, to plan what was now useless, to be the architect of the irrevocable past. Meanwhile, and behind all this activity, brute terrors, like the scurrying of rats in a deserted attic, filled the more remote chambers of his brain with riot; the hand of the constable would fall heavy on his shoulder, and his nerves would jerk like a hooked fish; or he beheld, in galloping defile, the dock, the prison, the gallows, and the black coffin.

Terror of the people in the street sat down before his mind like a besieging army. It was impossible, he thought, but that some rumour of the struggle must have reached their ears and set on edge their curiosity; and now, in all the neighbouring houses, he divined them sitting motionless and with uplifted ear - solitary people, condemned to spend Christmas dwelling alone on memories of the past, and now startingly recalled from that tender exercise; happy family parties struck into silence round the table, the mother still with raised finger - every degree and age and humour, but all, by their own hearths, prying and hearkening and weaving the rope that was to hang him. Sometimes it seemed to him he could not move too softly; the clink of the tall Bohemian goblets rang out loudly like a bell; and alarmed by the bigness of the ticking, he was tempted to stop the clocks. And then, again, with a swift transition of his terrors, the very silence of the place appeared a source of peril, and a thing to strike and freeze the passer-by; and he would step more boldly, and bustle aloud among the contents of the shop, and imitate, with elaborate bravado, the movements of a busy man at ease in his own house.

But he was now so pulled about by different alarms that, while one portion of his mind was still alert and cunning, another trembled on the brink of lunacy. One hallucination in particular took a strong hold on his credulity. The neighbour hearkening with white face beside his window, the passer-by arrested by a horrible surmise on the pavement - these could at worst suspect, they could not know; through the brick walls and shuttered windows only sounds could penetrate. But here, within the house, was he alone? He knew he was; he had watched the servant set forth sweet-hearting, in her poor best, "out for the day" written in every ribbon and smile. Yes, he was alone, of course; and yet, in the bulk of empty house above him, he could surely hear a stir of delicate footing; he was surely conscious, inexplicably conscious of some presence. Ay, surely; to every room and corner of the house his imagination followed it; and now it was a faceless thing, and yet had eyes to see with; and again it was a shadow of himself; and yet again behold the image of the dead dealer, reinspired with cunning and hatred.

At times, with a strong effort, he would glance at the open door which still seemed to repel his eyes. The house was tall, the skylight small and dirty, the day blind with fog; and the light that filtered down to the ground story was exceedingly faint, and showed dimly on the threshold of the shop. And yet, in that strip of doubtful brightness, did there not hang wavering a shadow?

Suddenly, from the street outside, a very jovial gentleman began to beat with a staff on the shop door, accompanying his blows with shouts and railleries in which the dealer was continually called upon by name. Markheim, smitten into ice, glanced at the dead man. But no! he lay quite still; he was fled away far beyond earshot of these blows and shoutings; he was sunk beneath seas of silence; and his name, which would once have caught his notice above the howling of a storm, had become an empty sound. And presently the jovial gentleman desisted from his knocking and departed.

Here was a broad hint to hurry what remained to be done, to get forth from this accusing neighbourhood, to plunge into a bath of London multitudes, and to reach, on the other side of day, that haven of safety and apparent innocence - his bed. One visitor had come; at any moment another might follow and be more obstinate. To have done the deed, and yet not to reap the profit, would be too abhorrent a failure. The money - that was now Markheim's concern; and as a means to that, the keys.

He glanced over his shoulder at the open door, where the shadow was still lingering and shivering; and with no conscious repugnance of the mind, yet with a tremor of the belly, he drew near the body of his victim. The human character had quite departed. Like a suit half-stuffed with bran, the limbs lay scattered, the trunk doubled, on the floor; and yet the thing repelled him. Although so dingy and inconsiderable to the eye, he feared it might have more significance to the touch. He took the body by the shoulders, and turned it on its back. It was strangely light and supple, and the limbs, as if they had been broken, fell into the oddest postures. The face was robbed of all expression; but it was as pale as wax, and shockingly smeared with blood about one temple. That was, for Markheim, the one displeasing circumstance. It carried him back, upon the instant, to a certain fair-day in a fishers' village: a gray day, a piping wind, a crowd upon the street, the blare of brasses, the booming of drums, the nasal voice of a ballad singer; and a boy going to and fro, buried overhead in the crowd and divided between interest and fear, until, coming out upon the chief place of concourse, he beheld a booth and a great screen with pictures, dismally designed, garishly coloured – Brownrigg with her apprentice, the Mannings with their murdered guest, Weare in the death-grip of Thurtell, and a score besides of famous crimes. The thing was as clear as an illusion He was once again that little boy; he was looking once again, and with the same sense of physical revolt, at these vile pictures; he was still stunned by the thumping of the drums. A bar of that day's music returned upon his memory; and at that, for the first time, a qualm came over him, a breath of nausea, a sudden weakness of the joints, which he must instantly resist and conquer.

He judged it more prudent to confront than to flee from these considerations, looking the more hardily in the dead face, bending his mind to realise the nature and greatness of his crime. So little a while ago that face had moved with every change of sentiment, that pale mouth had spoken, that body had been all on fire with governable energies; and now, and by his act, that piece of life had been arrested, as the horologist, with interjected finger, arrests the beating of the clock. So he reasoned in vain; he could rise to no more remorseful consciousness; the same heart which had shuddered before the painted effigies of crime, looked on its reality unmoved. At best, he felt a gleam of pity for one who had been endowed in vain with all those faculties that can make the world a garden of enchantment, one who had never lived and who was now dead. But of penitence, no, not a tremor.

With that, shaking himself clear of these considerations, he found the keys and advanced toward the open door of the shop. Outside, it had begun to rain smartly, and the sound of the shower upon the roof had banished silence. Like some dripping cavern, the chambers of the house were haunted by an incessant echoing, which filled the ear and mingled with the ticking of the clocks. And, as Markheim approached the door, he seemed to hear, in answer to his own cautious tread, the steps of another foot withdrawing up the stair. The shadow still palpitated loosely on the threshold. He threw a ton's weight of resolve upon his muscles, and drew back the door.

The faint, foggy daylight glimmered dimly on the bare floor and stairs; on the bright suit of armour posted, halbert in hand, upon the landing; and on the dark wood-carvings, and framed pictures that hung against the yellow panels of the wainscot. So loud was the beating of the rain through all the house that, in Markheim's ears, it began to be distinguished into many different sounds. Footsteps and sighs, the tread of regiments marching in the distance, the chink of money in the counting, and the creaking of doors held stealthily ajar, appeared to mingle with the patter of the drops upon the cupola and the gushing of the water in the pipes. The sense that he was not alone grew upon him to the verge of madness. On every side he was haunted and begirt by presences. He heard them moving in the upper chambers; from the shop, he heard the dead man getting to his legs; and as he began with a great effort to mount the stairs, feet fled quietly before him and followed stealthily behind. If he were but deaf, he thought, how tranquilly he would possess his soul! And then again, and hearkening with ever fresh attention, he blessed himself for that unresting sense which held the outposts and stood a trusty sentinel upon his life. His head turned continually on his neck; his eyes, which seemed starting from their orbits, scouted on every side, and on every side were half rewarded as with the tail of something nameless vanishing. The four and twenty steps to the first floor were four and twenty agonies.

On that first story, the doors stood ajar - three of them, like three ambushes, shaking his nerves like the throats of cannon. He could never again, he felt, be sufficiently immured and fortified from men's observing eyes; he longed to be home, girt in by walls, buried among bedclothes, and invisible to all but God. And at that thought he wondered a little, recollecting tales of other murderers and the fear they were said to entertain of heavenly avengers. It was not so, at least, with him. He feared the laws of nature, lest, in their callous and immutable procedure, they should preserve some damning evidence of his crime. He feared tenfold more, with a slavish, superstitious terror, some scission in the continuity of man's experience, some wilful illegality of nature. He played a game of skill, depending on the rules, calculating consequence from cause; and what if nature, as the defeated tyrant overthrew the chess-board, should break the mould of their succession? The like had befallen Napoleon (so writers said) when the winter changed the time of its appearance. The like might befall Markheim: the solid walls might become transparent and reveal his doings like those of bees in a glass hive; the stout planks might yield under his foot like quicksands and detain him in their clutch. Ay, and there were soberer accidents that might destroy him; if, for instance, the house should fall and imprison him beside the body of his victim, or the house next door should fly on fire, and the firemen invade him from all sides. These things he feared; and, in a sense, these things might be called the hands of God reached forth against sin. But about God himself he was at ease; his act was doubtless exceptional, but so were his excuses, which God knew; it was there, and not among men, that he felt sure of justice.

When he had got safe into the drawing-room, and shut the door behind him, he was aware of a respite from alarms. The room was quite dismantled, uncarpeted besides, and strewn with packing-cases and incongruous furniture; several great pier-glasses, in which he beheld himself at various angles, like an actor on a stage; many pictures, framed and unframed, standing, with their faces to the wall; a fine Sheraton sideboard, a cabinet of marquetry, and a great old bed, with tapestry hangings. The windows opened to the floor; but by great good fortune the lower part of the shutters had been closed, and this concealed him from the neighbours. Here, then, Markheim drew in a packing-case before the cabinet, and began to search among the keys. It was a long business, for there were many; and it was irksome, besides; for, after all, there might be nothing in the cabinet, and time was on the wing. But the closeness of the occupation sobered him. With the tail of his eye he saw the door - even glanced at it from time to time directly, like a besieged commander pleased to verify the good estate of his defences. But in truth he was at peace. The rain falling in the street sounded natural and pleasant. Presently, on the other side, the notes of a piano were wakened to the music of a hymn, and the voices of many children took up the air and words. How stately, how comfortable was the melody! How fresh the youthful voices! Markheim gave ear to it smilingly, as he sorted out the keys; and his mind was thronged with answerable ideas and images: church-going children, and the pealing of the high organ; children afield, bathers by the brookside, ramblers on the brambly common, kite-flyers in the windy and cloud-navigated sky; and then, at another cadence of the hymn, back again to church, and the somnolence of summer Sundays, and the high genteel voice of the parson (which he smiled a little to recall) and the painted Jacobean tombs, and the dim lettering of the Ten Commandments in the chancel.

And as he sat thus, at once busy and absent, he was startled to his feet. A flash of ice, a flash of fire, a bursting gush of blood, went over him, and then he stood transfixed and thrilling. A step mounted the stair slowly and steadily, and presently a hand was laid upon the knob, and the lock clicked, and the door opened.

Fear held Markheim in a vice. What to expect he knew not - whether the dead man walking, or the official ministers of human justice, or some chance witness blindly stumbling in to consign him to the gallows. But when a face was thrust into the aperture, glanced round the room, looked at him, nodded and smiled as if in friendly recognition, and then withdrew again, and the door closed behind it, his fear broke loose from his control in a hoarse cry. At the sound of this the visitant returned.

"Did you call me?" he asked, pleasantly, and with that he entered the room and closed the door behind him.

Markheim stood and gazed at him with all his eyes. Perhaps there was a film upon his sight, but the outlines of the new comer seemed to change and waver like those of the idols in the wavering candle-light of the shop; and at times he thought he knew him; and at times he thought he bore a likeness to himself; and always, like a lump of living terror, there lay in his bosom the conviction that this thing was not of the earth and not of God.

And yet the creature had a strange air of the common-place, as he stood looking on Markheim with a smile; and when he added, "You are looking for the money, I believe?" it was in the tones of everyday politeness.

Markheim made no answer.

"I should warn you," resumed the other, "that the maid has left her sweetheart earlier than usual and will soon be here. If Mr. Markheim be found in this house, I need not describe to him the consequences."

"You know me?" cried the murderer.

The visitor smiled. "You have long been a favourite of mine," he said; "and I have long observed and often sought to help you."

"What are you?" cried Markheim; "the devil?"

"What I may be," returned the other, "cannot affect the service I propose to render you."

"It can," cried Markheim; "it does! Be helped by you? No, never; not by you! You do not know me yet; thank God, you do not know me!"

"I know you," replied the visitant, with a sort of kind severity or rather firmness. "I know you to the soul."

"Know me!" cried Markheim. "Who can do so? My life is but a travesty and slander on myself. I have lived to belie my nature. All men do; all men are better than this disguise that grows about and stifles them. You see each dragged away by life, like one whom bravos have seized and muffled in a cloak. If they had their own control - if you could see their faces, they would be altogether different, they would shine out for heroes and saints! I am worse than most; myself is more overlaid; my excuse is known to me and God. But, had I the time, I could disclose myself."

"To me?" inquired the visitant.

"To you before all," returned the murderer. "I supposed you were intelligent. I thought - since you exist - you would prove a reader of the heart. And yet you would propose to judge me by my acts! Think of it - my acts! I was born and I have lived in a land of giants; giants have dragged me by the wrists since I was born out of my mother - the giants of circumstance. And you would judge me by my acts! But can you not look within? Can you not understand that evil is hateful to me? Can you not see within me the clear writing of conscience, never blurred by any wilful sophistry, although too often disregarded? Can you not read me for a thing that surely must be common as humanity - the unwilling sinner?" "All this is very feelingly expressed," was the reply, "but it regards me not. These points of consistency are beyond my province, and I care not in the least by what compulsion you may have been dragged away, so as you are but carried in the right direction. But time flies; the servant delays, looking in the faces of the crowd and at the pictures on the hoardings, but still she keeps moving nearer; and remember, it is as if the gallows itself was striding towards you through the Christmas streets! Shall I help you - I, who know all? Shall I tell you where to find the money?"

"For what price?" asked Markheim.

"I offer you the service for a Christmas gift," returned the other.

Markheim could not refrain from smiling with a kind of bitter triumph. "No," said he, "I will take nothing at your hands; if I were dying of thirst, and it was your hand that put the pitcher to my lips, I should find the courage to refuse. It may be credulous, but I will do nothing to commit myself to evil."

"I have no objection to a death-bed repentance," observed the visitant.

"Because you disbelieve their efficacy!" Markheim cried.

"I do not say so," returned the other; "but I look on these things from a different side, and when the life is done my interest falls. The man has lived to serve me, to spread black looks under colour of religion, or to sow tares in the wheat-field, as you do, in a course of weak compliance with desire. Now that he draws so near to his deliverance, he can add but one act of service: to repent, to die smiling, and thus to build up in confidence and hope the more timorous of my surviving followers. I am not so hard a master. Try me; accept my help. Please yourself in life as you have done hitherto; please yourself more amply, spread your elbows at the board; and when the night begins to fall and the curtains to be drawn, I tell you, for your greater comfort, that you will find it even easy to compound your quarrel with your conscience, and to make a truckling peace with God. I came but now from such a death-bed, and the room was full of sincere mourners, listening to the man's last words; and when I looked into that face, which had been set as a flint against mercy, I found it smiling with hope."

"And do you, then, suppose me such a creature?" asked Markheim. "Do you think I have no more generous aspirations than to sin and sin and sin and at last sneak into heaven? My heart rises at the thought. Is this, then, your experience of mankind? or is it because you find me with red hands that you presume such baseness? And is this crime of murder indeed so impious as to dry up the very springs of good?"

"Murder is to me no special category," replied the other. "All sins are murder, even as all life is war. I behold your race, like starving mariners on a raft, plucking crusts out of the hands of famine and feeding on each other's lives. I follow sins beyond the moment of their acting; I find in all that the last consequence is death, and to my eyes, the pretty maid who thwarts her mother with such taking graces on a question of a ball, drips no less visibly with human gore than such a murderer as yourself. Do I say that I follow sins? I follow virtues also. They differ not by the thickness of a nail; they are both scythes for the reaping angel of Death. Evil, for which I live, consists not in action but in character. The bad man is dear to me, not the bad act, whose fruits, if we could follow them far enough down the hurtling cataract of the ages, might yet be found more blessed than those of the rarest virtues. And it is not because you have killed a dealer, but because you are Markheim, that I offer to forward your escape."

"I will lay my heart open to you," answered Markheim. "This crime on which you find me is my last. On my way to it I have learned many lessons; itself is a lesson - a momentous lesson. Hitherto I have been driven with revolt to what I would not; I was a bond-slave to poverty, driven and scourged. There are robust virtues that can stand in these temptations; mine was not so; I had a thirst of pleasure. But to-day, and out of this deed, I pluck both warning and riches - both the power and a fresh resolve to be myself. I become in all things a free actor in the world; I begin to see myself all changed, these hands the agents of good, this heart at peace. Something comes over me out of the past - something of what I have dreamed on Sabbath evenings to the sound of the church organ, of what I forecast when I shed tears over noble books, or talked, an innocent child, with my mother. There lies my life; I have wandered a few years, but now I see once more my city of destination."

"You are to use this money on the Stock Exchange, I think?" remarked the visitor; "and there, if I mistake not, you have already lost some thousands?"

"Ah," said Markheim, "but this time I have a sure thing."

"This time, again, you will lose," replied the visitor quietly.

"Ah, but I keep back the half!" cried Markheim.

"That also you will lose," said the other.

The sweat started upon Markheim's brow. "Well then, what matter?" he exclaimed. "Say it be lost, say I am plunged again in poverty, shall one part of me, and that the worse, continue until the end to override the better? Evil and good run strong in me, hailing me both ways. I do not love the one thing; I love all. I can conceive great deeds, renunciations, martyrdoms; and though I be fallen to such a crime as murder, pity is no stranger to my thoughts. I pity the poor; who knows their trials better than myself? I pity and help them. I prize love; I love honest laughter; there is no good thing nor true thing on earth but I love it from my heart. And are my vices only to direct my life, and my virtues to lie without effect, like some passive lumber of the mind? Not so; good, also, is a spring of acts."

But the visitant raised his finger. "For six and thirty years that you have been in this world," said he, "through many changes of fortune and varieties of humour, I have watched you steadily fall. Fifteen years ago you would have started at a theft. Three years back you would have blenched at the name of murder. Is there any crime, is there any cruelty or meanness, from which you still recoil? Five years from now I shall detect you in the fact! Downward, downward, lies your way; nor can anything but death avail to stop you."

"It is true," Markheim said huskily, "I have in some degree complied with evil. But it is so with all; the very saints, in the mere exercise of living, grow less dainty, and take on the tone of their surroundings."

"I will propound to you one simple question," said the other; "and as you answer I shall read to you your moral horoscope. You have grown in many things more lax; possibly you do right to be so; and at any account, it is the same with all men. But granting that, are you in any one particular, however trifling, more difficult to please with your own conduct, or do you go in all things with a looser rein?"

"In any one?" repeated Markheim, with an anguish of consideration. "No," he added, with despair; "in none! I have gone down in all."

"Then," said the visitor, "content yourself with what you are, for you will never change; and the words of your part on this stage are irrevocably written down."

Markheim stood for a long while silent, and, indeed, it was the visitor who first broke the silence. "That being so," he said, "shall I show you the money?"

"And grace?" cried Markheim.

"Have you not tried it?" returned the other. "Two or three years ago did I not see you on the platform of revival meetings, and was not your voice the loudest in the hymn?"

"It is true," said Markheim; "and I see clearly what remains for me by way of duty. I thank you for these lessons from my soul; my eyes are opened, and I behold myself at last for what I am."

At this moment, the sharp note of the door-bell rang through the house; and the visitant, as though this were some concerted signal for which he had been waiting, changed at once in his demeanour.

"The maid!" he cried. "She has returned, as I forewarned you, and there is now before you one more difficult passage. Her master, you must say, is ill; you must let her in, with an assured but rather serious countenance; no smiles, no overacting, and I promise you success! Once the girl within, and the door closed, the same dexterity that has already rid you of the dealer will relieve you of this last danger in your path. Thenceforward you have the whole evening - the whole night, if needful - to ransack the treasures of the house and to make good your safety. This is help that comes to you with the mask of danger. Up!" he cried; "up, friend. Your life hangs trembling in the scales; up, and act!"

Markheim steadily regarded his counsellor. "If I be condemned to evil acts," he said, "there is still one door of freedom open: I can cease from action. If my life be an ill thing, I can lay it down. Though I be, as you say truly, at the beck of every small temptation, I can yet, by one decisive gesture, place myself beyond the reach of all. My love of good is damned to barrenness; it may, and let it be! But I have still my hatred of evil; and from that, to your galling disappointment, you shall see that I can draw both energy and courage."

The features of the visitor began to undergo a wonderful and lovely change: they brightened and softened with a tender triumph, and, even as they brightened, faded and dislimned. But Markheim did not pause to watch or understand the transformation. He opened the door and went downstairs very slowly, thinking to himself. His past went soberly before him; he beheld it as it was, ugly and strenuous like a dream, random as chance medley - a scene of defeat. Life, as he thus reviewed it, tempted him no longer; but on the further side he perceived a quiet haven for his bark. He paused in the passage, and looked into the shop, where the candle still burned by the dead body. It was strangely silent. Thoughts of the dealer swarmed into his mind, as he stood gazing. And then the bell once more broke out into impatient clamour.

He confronted the maid upon the threshold with something like a smile.

"You had better go for the police," said he; "I have killed your master."

# QUEEN TITA'S WAGER

## I
## FRANZISKA FAHLER

It is a Christmas morning in Surrey - cold, still and gray, with a frail glimmer of sunshine coming through the bare trees to melt the hoar-frost on the lawn. The postman has just gone out, swinging the gate behind him. A fire burns brightly in the breakfast-room; and there is silence about the house, for the children have gone off to climb Box Hill before being marched to church.

The small and gentle lady who presides over the household walks sedately in, and lifts the solitary letter that is lying on her plate. About three seconds suffice to let her run through its contents, and then she suddenly cries:

"I knew it! I said it! I told you two months ago she was only flirting with him; and now she has rejected him. And oh! I am so glad of it! The poor boy!"

The other person in the room, who had been meekly waiting for his breakfast for half an hour, ventures to point out that there is nothing to rejoice over in the fact of a young man having been rejected by a young woman.

"If it were final, yes! If these two young folks were not certain to go and marry somebody else, you might congratulate them both. But you know they will. The poor boy will go courting again in three months' time, and be vastly pleased with his condition."

"Oh, never, never!" she says. "He has had such a lesson! You know I warned him. I knew she was only flirting with him. Poor Charlie! Now I hope he will get on with his profession, and leave such things out of his head. And as for that creature - "

"I will do you the justice to say," observes her husband, who is still regarding the table with a longing eye, "that you did oppose this match, because you hadn't the making of it. If you had brought these two together they would have been married ere this. Never mind; you can marry him to somebody of your own choosing now."

"No," she says, with much decision; "he must not think of marriage. He cannot think of it. It will take the poor lad a long time to get over this blow."

"He will marry within a year."

"I will bet you whatever you like that he doesn't," she says, triumphantly.

"Whatever I like! That is a big wager. If you lose, do you think you could pay? I should like, for example, to have my own way in my own house."

"If I lose you shall," says the generous creature; and the bargain is concluded.

Nothing further is said about this matter for the moment. The children return from Box Hill, and are rigged out for church. Two young people, friends of ours, and recently married, having no domestic circle of their own, and having promised to spend the whole Christmas Day with us, arrived. Then we set out, trying as much as possible to think that Christmas Day is different from any other day, and pleased to observe that the younger folk, at least, cherish the delusion.

But just before reaching the church I say to the small lady who got the letter in the morning, and whom we generally call Tita:

"When do you expect to see Charlie?"

"I don't know," she answers. "After this cruel affair he won't like to go about much."

"You remember that he promised to go with us to the Black Forest?"

"Yes; and I am sure it will be a pleasant trip for him."

"Shall we go to Huferschingen?"

"I suppose so."

"Franziska is a pretty girl."

Now you would not think that any great mischief could be done by the mere remark that Franziska was a pretty girl. Anybody who had seen Franziska Fahler, niece of the proprietor of the "Goldenen Bock" in Huferschingen, would admit that in a moment. But this is nevertheless true, that our important but diminutive

Queen Tita was very thoughtful during the rest of our walk to this little church; and in church, too, she was thinking so deeply that she almost forgot to look at the effect of the decorations she had nailed up the day before. Yet nothing could have offended in the bare observation that Franziska was a pretty girl.

At dinner in the evening we had our two guests and a few young fellows from London who did not happen to have their families or homes there. Curiously enough, there was a vast deal of talk about travelling, and also about Baden, and more particularly about the southern districts of Baden. Tita said the Black Forest was the most charming place in the world; and as it was Christmas Day, and as we had been listening to a sermon all about charity and kindness and consideration for others, nobody was rude enough to contradict her. But our forbearance was put to a severe test when, after dinner, she produced a photographic album and handed it round, and challenged everybody to say whether the young lady in the corner was not absolutely lovely. Most of them said that she was certainly very nice-looking; and Tita seemed a little disappointed.

I perceived that it would no longer do to say that Franziska was a pretty girl. We should henceforth have to swear by everything we held dear that she was absolutely lovely.

## II
## ZUM "GOLDENEN BOCK"

We felt some pity for the lad when we took him abroad with us; but it must be confessed that at first he was not a very desirable travelling companion. There was a gloom about him. Despite the eight months that had elapsed, he professed that his old wound was still open. Tita treated him with the kindest maternal solicitude, which was a great mistake; tonics, not sweets, are required in such cases. Yet he was very grateful, and he said, with a blush, that, in any case, he would not rail against all women because of the badness of one. Indeed, you would not have fancied he had any great grudge against womankind. There were a great many English abroad that autumn, and we met whole batches of pretty girls at every station and at every table d'hote on our route. Did he avoid them, or glare at them savagely, or say hard things of them? Oh no! quite the reverse. He was a little shy at first; and when he saw a party of distressed damsels in a station, with their bewildered father in vain attempting to make himself understood to a porter, he would assist them in a brief and businesslike manner as if it were a duty, lift his cap, and then march off relieved. But by-and-by he began to make acquaintances in the hotel; and as he was a handsome, English-looking lad, who bore a certificate of honesty in his clear gray eyes and easy gait, he was rather made much of. Nor could any fault be decently found with his appetite.

So we passed on from Konigswinter to Coblenz, and

from Coblenz to Heidelberg, and from Heidelberg south to Freiburg, where we bade adieu to the last of the towns, and laid hold of a trap with a pair of ancient and angular horses, and plunged into the Hollenthal, the first great gorge of the Black Forest mountains. From one point to another we slowly urged our devious course, walking the most of the day, indeed, and putting the trap and ourselves up for the night at some quaint roadside hostelry, where we ate of roe-deer and drank of Affenthaler, and endeavoured to speak German with a pure Waldshut accent. And then, one evening, when the last rays of the sun were shining along the hills and touching the stems of the tall pines, we drove into a narrow valley and caught sight of a large brown building of wood, with projecting eaves and quaint windows, that stood close by the forest.

"Here is my dear inn!" cried Tita, with a great glow of delight and affection in her face. "Here is mein gutes Thal! Ich gruss' dich ein tausend Mal! And here is old Peter come out to see us; and there is Franziska!"

"Oh, this is Franziska, is it?" said Charlie.

Yes, this was Franziska. She was a well-built, handsome girl of nineteen or twenty, with a healthy, sunburnt complexion, and dark hair plaited into two long tails, which were taken up and twisted into a knot behind. That you could see from a distance. But on nearer approach you found that Franziska had really fine and intelligent features, and a pair of frank, clear, big brown eyes that had a very straight look about them. They were something of the eyes of a deer, indeed; wide apart, soft, and apprehensive, yet looking with a certain directness and unconsciousness that overcame her natural girlish timidity. Tita simply flew at her and kissed her heartily and asked her twenty questions at once. Franziska answered in very fair English, a little slow and formal, but quite grammatical. Then she was introduced to Charlie, and she shook hands with him in a simple and unembarrassed way; and then she turned to one of the servants and gave some directions about the luggage. Finally she begged Tita to go indoors and get off her travelling attire, which was done, leaving us two outside.

"She's a very pretty girl," Charlie said, carelessly. "I suppose she's sort of head cook and kitchen-maid here."

The impudence of these young men is something extraordinary.

"If you wish to have your head in your hands," I remarked to him, "just you repeat that remark at dinner. Why, Franziska is no end of a swell. She has two thousand pounds and the half of a mill. She has a sister married to the Geheimer-Ober-Hofbaurath of Hesse-Cassel. She had visited both Paris and Munich, and she has her dresses made in Freiburg."

"But why does such an illustrious creature bury herself in this valley, and in an old inn, and go about bareheaded?"

"Because there are folks in the world without ambition, who like to live a quiet, decent, homely life. Every girl can't marry a Geheimer-Ober-Hofbaurath. Ziska, now, is much more likely to marry the young doctor here."

"Oh, indeed! and live here all her days. She couldn't do

better. Happy Franziska!"

We went indoors. It was a low, large, rambling place, with one immense room all hung round with roe-deers' horns, and with one lesser room fitted up with a billiard-table. The inn lay a couple of hundred yards back from Huferschingen; but it had been made the headquarters of the keepers, and just outside this room there were a number of pegs for them to sling their guns and bags on when they came in of an evening to have a pipe and a chopin of white wine. Ziska's uncle and aunt were both large, stout, and somnolent people, very good-natured and kind, but a trifle dull. Ziska really had the management of the place, and she was not slow to lend a hand if the servants were remiss in waiting on us. But that, it was understood, was done out of compliment to our small Queen Tita.

By-and-by we sat down to dinner, and Franziska came to see that everything was going on straight. It was a dinner "with scenery." You forgot to be particular about the soup, the venison, and the Affenthaler when from the window at your elbow you could look across the narrow valley and behold a long stretch of the Black Forest shining in the red glow of the sunset. The lower the sun sank the more intense became the crimson light on the tall stems of the pines; and then you could see the line of shadow slowly rising up the side of the opposite hill until only the topmost trees were touched with fire. Then these too lost it, and all the forest around us seemed to have a pale-blue mist stealing over it as the night fell and the twilight faded out of the sky overhead. Presently the long undulations of fir grew black, the stars came out, and the sound of the stream could be heard distantly in the hollow; and then, at Tita's wish, we went off for a last stroll in among the soft moss and under the darkness of the pines, now and again starting some great capercailzie, and sending it flying and whirring down the glades.

When we returned from that prowl into the forest, we found the inn dark. Such people as may have called in had gone home; but we suspected that Franziska had given the neighbours a hint not to overwhelm us on our first arrival. When we entered the big room, Franziska came in with candles; then she brought some matches, and also put on the table an odd little pack of cards, and went out. Her uncle and aunt had, even before we went out, come and bade us good-night formally, and shaken hands all round. They are early folk in the Black Forest.

"Where has that girl gone now?" says Charlie. "Into that lonely billiard-room! Couldn't you ask her to come in here? Or shall we go and play billiards?"

Tita stares, and then demurely smiles; but it is with an assumed severity that she rebukes him for such a wicked proposal, and reminds him that he must start early next morning. He groans assent. Then she takes her leave.

The big young man was silent for a moment or two, with his hands in his pockets and his legs stretched out. I begin to think I am in for it - the old story of blighted hopes and angry denunciation and hypocritical joy, and all the rest of it. But suddenly Charlie looks up with a businesslike air and says:

"Who is that doctor fellow you were speaking about! Shall we see him to-morrow?"

"You saw him to-night. It was he who passed us on the road with the two beagles."

"What! that little fellow with the bandy legs and the spectacles?" he cries, with a great laugh.

"That little fellow," I observe to him, "is a person of some importance, I can tell you. He - "

"I suppose his sister married a Geheimer-Ober-under - what the dickens is it?" says this disrespectful young man.

"Dr. Krumm has got the Iron Cross."

"That won't make his legs any the straighter."

"He was at Weissenburg."

"I suppose he got that cast in the eye there."

"He can play the zither in a way that would astonish you. He has got a little money. Franziska and he would be able to live very comfortably together."

"Franziska and that fellow?" says Charlie; and then he rises with a sulky air, and proposes we should take our candles with us.

But he is not sulky very long; for Ziska, hearing our footsteps, comes to the passage and bids us a friendly good-night.

"Good-night, Miss Fahler!" he says, in rather a shamefaced way; "and I am so awfully sorry we have kept you up so late. We sha'n't do it again."

You would have thought by his manner that it was two o'clock, whereas it was only half-past eleven!

## III
## DR. KRUMM

There was no particular reason why Dr. Krumm should marry Franziska Fahler, except that he was the most important young man in Huferschingen, and she was the most important young woman. People therefore thought they would make a good match, although Franziska certainly had the most to give in the way of good looks. Dr. Krumm was a short, bandy-legged, sturdy young man, with long, fair hair, a tanned complexion, light-blue eyes not quite looking the same way, spectacles, and a general air of industrious common sense about him, if one may use such a phrase. There was certainly little of the lover in his manner toward Ziska, and as little in hers toward him. They were very good friends, though, and he called her Ziska, while she gave him his nickname of Fidelio, his real name being Fidele.

Now on this, the first morning of our stay in Huferschingen, all the population had turned out at an early hour to see us start for the forest; and as the Ober-Forster had gone away to visit his parents in Bavaria, Dr. Krumm was appointed to superintend the operations of the day. And when everybody was busy renewing acquaintance with us, gathering the straying dogs, examining guns and cartridge-belts, and generally aiding in the profound commotion of our setting out, Dr. Krumm was found to be talking in a very friendly and familiar manner with our pretty Franziska. Charlie eyed them askance. He began to say disrespectful things of Krumm: he thought Krumm a plain person. And then, when the bandy-legged doctor had got all the dogs, keepers, and beaters together, we set off along the road, and presently plunged into the cool shade of the forest, where the thick moss suddenly silenced our footsteps, and where there was a moist and resinous smell in the air.

Well, the incidents of the forenoon's shooting, picturesque as they were, and full of novelty to Tita's protege, need not be described. At the end of the fourth drive, when we had got on nearly to luncheon-time, it appeared that Charlie had killed a handsome buck, and he was so pleased with this performance that he grew friendly with Dr. Krumm, who had, indeed, given him the /haupt-stelle/. But when, as we sat down to our sausages and bread and red wine, Charlie incidentally informed our commander-in-chief that, during one of the drives, a splendid yellow fox had come out of the underwood and stood and stared at him for three or four seconds, the doctor uttered a cry of despair.

"I should have told you that," he said, in English that was not quite so good as Ziska's, "if I had remembered, yes! The English will not shoot the foxes; but they are very bad for us; they kill the young deer. We are glad to shoot them; and Franziska she told me she wanted a yellow fox for the skin to make something."

Charlie got very red in the face. He had missed a chance. If he had known that Franziska wanted a yellow fox, all the instinctive veneration for that animal that was in him would have gone clean out, and the fate of the animal - for Charlie was a smart shot - would have been definitely sealed.

"Are there many of them?" said he, gloomily.

"No; not many. But where there is one there are generally four or five. In the next drive we may come on them, yes! I will put you in a good place, sir, and you must not think of letting him go away; for Franziska, who has waited two, three weeks, and not one yellow fox not anywhere, and it is for the variety of the skin in a - a - I do not know what you call it."

"A rug, I suppose," said Charlie.

I subsequently heard that Charlie went to his post with a fixed determination to shoot anything of yellow colour that came near him. His station was next to that of Dr. Krumm; but of course they were invisible to each other. The horns of the beaters sounded a warning; the gunners cocked their guns and stood on the alert; in the perfect silence each one waited for the first glimmer of a brown hide down the long green glades of young fir. Then, according to Charlie's account, by went two or three deer like lightning - all of them does. A buck came last, but swerved just as he came in sight, and backed and made straight for the line of beaters. Two more does, and then an absolute blank. One or two shots had been heard at a distance; either some of the more distant stations had been more fortunate, or one or other of the beaters had tried his luck. Suddenly there was a shot fired close to Charlie; he knew it must have been the doctor. In about a minute afterward he saw some pale-yellow object slowly worming its way through the ferns; and here, at length, he made sure he was going to get his yellow fox. But just as the animal came within fair distance, it turned over, made a struggle or two, and lay still. Charlie rushed along to the spot: it was, indeed, a yellow fox, shot in the head, and now as dead as a door-nail.

What was he to do? Let Dr. Krumm take home this prize to Franziska, after he had had such a chance in the afternoon? Never! Charlie fired a barrel into the air, and then calmly awaited the coming up of the beaters and the drawing together of the sportsmen.

Dr. Krumm, being at the next station, was the first to arrive. He found Charlie standing by the side of the slain fox.

"Ha!" he said, his spectacles fairly gleaming with delight, "you have shotted him! You have killed him! That is very good - that is excellent! Now you will present the skin to Miss Franziska, if you do not wish to take it to England."

"Oh no!" said Charlie, with a lordly indifference. "I don't care about it. Franziska may have it."

Charlie pulled me aside, and said, with a solemn wink:

"Can you keep a secret?"

"My wife and I can keep a secret. I am not allowed to have any for myself."

"Listen," said the unabashed young man; "Krumm shot that fox. Mind you don't say a word. I must have the skin to present to Franziska."

I stared at him; I had never known him guilty of a dishonest action. But when you do get a decent young English fellow condescending to do anything shabby, be sure it is a girl who is the cause. I said nothing, of course; and in the evening a trap came for us, and we drove back to Huferschingen.

Tita clapped her hands with delight; for Charlie was a favourite of hers, and now he was returning like a hero, with a sprig of fir in his cap to show that he had killed a buck.

"And here, Miss Franziska," he said, quite gaily, "here is a yellow fox for you. I was told that you wanted the skin of one."

Franziska fairly blushed for pleasure; not that the skin of a fox was very valuable for her, but that the compliment was so open and marked. She came forward, in German fashion, and rather shyly shook hands with him in token of her thanks.

When Tita was getting ready for dinner I told her about the yellow fox. A married man must have no secrets.

"He is not capable of such a thing," she says, with a grand air.

"But he did it," I point out. "What is more, he glories in it. What did he say when I remonstrated with him on the way home! 'Why,' says he, 'I will put an end to Krumm! I will abolish Krumm! I will extinguish Krumm!' Now, madame, who is responsible for this? Who had been praising Franziska night and day as the sweetest, gentlest, cleverest girl in the world, until this young man determines to have a flirtation with her and astonish you?"

"A flirtation!" says Tita, faintly. "Oh no! Oh, I never

meant that."

"Ask him just now, and he will tell you that women deserve no better. They have no hearts; they are treacherous. They have beautiful eyes, but no conscience. And so he means to take them as they are, and have his measure of amusement."

"Oh, I am sure he never said anything so abominably wicked," cried Tita, laying down the rose that Franziska had given her for her hair. "I know he could not say such things. But if he is so wicked - if he has said them - it is not too late to interfere. I will see about it."

She drew herself up as if Jupiter had suddenly armed her with his thunderbolts. If Charlie had seen her at this moment he would have quailed. He might by chance have told the truth, and confessed that all the wicked things he had been saying about woman's affection were only a sort of rhetoric, and that he had no sort of intention to flirt with poor Franziska, nor yet to extinguish and annihilate Dr. Krumm.

The heartbroken boy was in very good spirits at dinner. He was inclined to wink. Tita, on the contrary, maintained an impressive dignity of demeanour; and when Franziska's name happened to be mentioned she spoke of the young girl as her very particular friend, as though she would dare Charlie to attempt a flirtation with one who held that honour. But the young man was either blind or reckless, or acting a part for mere mischief. He pointed the finger of scorn at Dr. Krumm. He asked Tita if he should bring her a yellow fox next day. He declared he wished he could spend the remainder of his life in a Black Forest Inn, with a napkin over his arm, serving chopins. He said he would brave the wrath of the Furst by shooting a capercailzie on the very first opportunity, to bring the shining feathers home to Franziska.

When Tita and I went upstairs at night the small and gentle creature was grievously perplexed.

"I cannot make it out," she said. "He is quite changed. What is the matter with him?"

"You behold, madam, in that young man the moral effects of vulpicide. A demon has entered into him. You remember, in 'Der Freischutz,' how - "

"Did you say vulpicide?" she asks, with a sweet smile. "I understood that Charlie's crime was that he did not kill the fox."

I allow her the momentary triumph. Who would grudge to a woman a little verbal victory of that sort? And, indeed, Tita's satisfaction did not last long. Her perplexity became visible on her face once more.

"We are to be here three weeks," she said, almost to herself, "and he talks of flirting with poor Franziska. Oh, I never meant that!"

"But what did you mean?" I ask her, with innocent wonder.

Tita hangs down her head, and there is an end to that conversation; but one of us, at least, has some recollection of a Christmas wager.

## IV
## CONFESSIO AMANTIS

Charlie was not in such good spirits next morning. He was standing outside the inn, in the sweet, resinous-scented air, watching Franziska coming and going, with her bright face touched by the early sunlight, and her frank and honest eyes lit up by a kindly look when she passed us. His conscience began to smite him for claiming that fox.

We spent the day in fishing a stream some few miles distant from Huferschingen, and Franziska accompanied us. What need to tell of our success with the trout and the grayling, or of the beautiful weather, or of the attentive and humble manner in which the unfortunate youth addressed Franziska from time to time?

In the evening we drove back to Huferschingen. It was a still and beautiful evening, with the silence of the twilight falling over the lonely valleys and the miles upon miles of darkening pines. Charlie has not much of a voice, but he made an effort to sing with Tita:

> "The winds whistle cold and the stars glimmer red,
> The sheep are in fold and the cattle in shed;"

and the fine old glee sounded fairly well as we drove through the gathering gloom of the forest. But Tita sang, in her low, sweet fashion, that Swedish bridal song that begins:

"Oh, welcome her so fair, with bright and flowing hair;
May Fate through life befriend her, love and smiles
attend her;"

and though she sang quietly, just as if she were singing to herself, we all listened with great attention, and with great gratitude too. When we got out of Huferschingen, the stars were out over the dark stretches of forest, and the windows of the quaint old inn were burning brightly.

"And have you enjoyed the amusement of the day?" says Miss Fahler, rather shyly, to a certain young man who is emptying his creel of fish. He drops the basket to turn round and look at her face and say earnestly:

"I have never spent so delightful a day; but it wasn't the fishing."

Things were becoming serious.

And next morning Charlie got hold of Tita, and said to her, in rather a shamefaced way:

"What am I to do about that fox? It was only a joke, you know; but if Miss Fahler gets to hear of it, she'll think it was rather shabby."

It was always Miss Fahler now; a couple of days before it was Franziska.

"For my part," says Tita, "I can't understand why you did it. What honour is there in shooting a fox?"

"But I wanted to give the skin to her."

It was "her" by this time.

"Well, I think the best thing you can do is to go and tell her all about it; and also to go and apologise to Dr. Krumm."

Charlie started.

"I will go and tell her, certainly; but as for apologising to Krumm, that is absurd!"

"As you please," says Tita.

By-and-by Franziska - or rather Miss Fahler - came out of the small garden and round by the front of the house.

"O Miss Fahler," says Charlie, suddenly, - and with that she stops and blushes slightly, - "I've got something to say to you. I am going to make a confession. Don't be frightened; it's only about a fox - the fox that was brought home the day before yesterday; Dr. Krumm shot that."

"Indeed," says Franziska, quite innocently, "I thought you shot it."

"Well, I let them imagine so. It was only a joke."

"But it is of no matter; there are many yellow foxes. Dr. Krumm can shoot them at another time; he is always here. Perhaps you will shoot one before you go."

With that Franziska passed into the house, carrying her fruit with her. Charlie was left to revolve her words in his mind. Dr. Krumm could shoot foxes when he chose; he was always here. He, Charlie, on the contrary, had to go away in little more than a fortnight. There was no Franziska in England; no pleasant driving through great pine woods in the gathering twilight; no shooting of yellow foxes, to be brought home in triumph and presented to a beautiful and grateful young woman. Charlie walked along the white road and overtook Tita, who had just sat down on a little camp-stool, and got out the materials for taking a water-colour sketch of the Huferschingen Valley. He sat down at her feet on the warm grass.

"I suppose I sha'n't interrupt your painting by talking to you?" he says.

"Oh dear, no," is the reply; and then he begins, in a somewhat hesitating way, to ask indirect questions and drop hints and fish for answers, just as if this small creature, who was busy with her sepias and olive greens, did not see through all this transparent cunning.

At last she said to him, frankly:

"You want me to tell you whether Franziska would make a good wife for you. She would make a good wife for any man. But then you seem to think that I should intermeddle and negotiate and become a go-between. How can I do that. My husband is always accusing me of trying to make up matches; and you know that isn't true."

"I know it isn't true," says the hypocrite; "but you might only this once. I believe all you say about this girl; I can see it for myself; and when shall I ever have such a chance again?"

"But dear me!" says Tita, putting down the white palette for a moment, "how can I believe you are in earnest? You have only known her three days."

"And that is quite enough," says Charlie, boldly, "to let you find out all you want to know about a girl if she is of the right sort. If she isn't you won't find out in three years. Now look at Franziska; look at the fine, intelligent face and the honest eyes; you can have no doubt about her; and then I have all the guarantee of your long acquaintance with her."

"Oh," says Tita, "that is all very well. Franziska is an excellent girl, as I have told you often - frank, kind, well educated, and unselfish. But you cannot have fallen in love with her in three days?"

"Why not?" says this blunt-spoken young man.

"Because it is ridiculous. If I meddle in the affair I should probably find you had given up the fancy in other three days; or if you did marry her and took her to England you would get to hate me because I alone should know that you had married the niece of an innkeeper."

"Well, I like that!" says he, with a flush in his face. "Do you think I should care two straws whether my friends knew I had married the niece of an innkeeper? I should show them Franziska. Wouldn't that be enough? An innkeeper's niece! I wish the world had more of 'em, if they're like Franziska."

"And besides," says Tita, "have you any notion as to how Franziska herself would probably take this mad proposal?"

"No," says the young man, humbly. "I wanted you to try and find out what she thought about me; and if, in time something were said about this proposal, you might put in a word or two, you know, just to - to give her an idea, you know, that you don't think it quite so mad, don't you know?"

"Give me your hand, Charlie," says Tita, with a sudden burst of kindness. "I'll do what I can for you; for I know she's a good girl, and she will make a good wife to the man who marries her."

You will observe that this promise was given by a lady who never, in any circumstances whatsoever, seeks to make up matches, who never speculates on possible combinations when she invites young people to her house in Surrey, and who is profoundly indignant, indeed, when such a charge is preferred against her. Had she not, on that former Christmas morning, repudiated with scorn the suggestion that Charlie might marry before another year had passed? Had she not, in her wild confidence, staked on a wager that assumption of authority in her household and out of it without which life would be a burden to her? Yet no sooner was the name of Franziska mentioned, and no sooner had she been reminded that Charlie was going with us to Huferschingen, than the nimble little brain set to work. Oftentimes it has occurred to one dispassionate spectator of her ways that this same Tita resembled the small object which, thrown into a dish of some liquid chemical substance, suddenly produces a mass of crystals. The constituents of those beautiful combinations, you see, were there; but they wanted some little shock to hasten the slow process of crystallisation. Now in our social circle we have continually observed groups of young people floating about in an amorphous and chaotic fashion - good for nothing but dawdling through dances, and flirting, and carelessly separating again; but when you dropped Tita among them, then you would see how rapidly this jellyfish sort of existence was abolished - how the groups got broken up, and how the sharp, businesslike relations of marriage were precipitated and made permanent. But would she own to it? Never! She once went and married her dearest friend to a Prussian officer; and now she declares he was a selfish fellow to carry off the girl in that way, and rates him soundly because he won't bring her to stay with us more than three months out of the twelve. There are some of us get quite enough of this Prussian occupation of our territory.

"Well," says Tita to this long English lad, who is lying sprawling on the grass, "I can safely tell you this, that Franziska likes you very well."

He suddenly jumps up, and there is a great blush on his face.

"Has she said so?" he asks, eagerly.

"Oh yes! in a way. She thinks you are good-natured. She likes the English generally. She asked me if that ring you wear was an engaged ring."

These disconnected sentences were dropped with a tantalising slowness into Charlie's eager ears.

"I must go and tell her directly that it is not," said he; and he might probably have gone off at once had not Tita restrained him.

"You must be a great deal more cautious than that if you wish to carry off Franziska some day or other. If you were to ask her to marry you now she would flatly refuse you, and very properly; for how could a girl believe you were in earnest? But if you like, Charlie, I will say something to her that will give her a hint; and if she cares for you at all before you go away she won't forget you. I wish I was as sure of you as I am of her."

"Oh I can answer for myself," says the young man, with a becoming bashfulness.

Tita was very happy and pleased all that day. There was an air of mystery and importance about her. I knew what it meant; I had seen it before.

Alas! poor Charlie!

## V
## "GAB MIR EIN' RING DABEI"

Under the friendly instructions of Dr. Krumm, whom he no longer regarded as a possible rival, Charlie became a mighty hunter; and you may be sure that he returned of an evening with sprigs of fir in his cap for the bucks he had slain, Franziska was not the last to come forward and shake hands with him and congratulate him, as is the custom in these primitive parts. And then she was quite made one of the family when we sat down to dinner in the long, low-roofed room; and nearly every evening, indeed, Tita would have her to dine with us and play cards with us.

You may suppose, if these two young folk had any regard for each other, those evenings in the inn must have been a pleasant time for them. There were never two partners at whist who were so courteous to each other, so charitable to each other's blunders. Indeed, neither would ever admit that the other blundered. Charlie used to make some frightful mistakes occasionally that would have driven any other player mad; but you should have seen the manner in which Franziska would explain that he had no alternative but to take her king with his ace, that he could not know this, and was right in chancing that. We played three-penny points, and Charlie paid for himself and his partner, in spite of her entreaties. Two of us found the game of whist a profitable thing.

One day a registered letter came for Charlie. He seized

it, carried it to a window, and then called Tita to him. Why need he have any secret about it? It was nothing but a ring - a plain hoop with a row of rubies.

"Do you think she would take this thing?" he said, in a low voice.

"How can I tell?"

The young man blushed and stammered, and said:

"I don't want you to ask her to take the ring, but to get to know whether she would accept any present from me. And I would ask her myself plainly, only you have been frightening me so much about being in a hurry. And what am I to do? Three days hence we start."

Tita looked down with a smile and said, rather timidly:

"I think if I were you I would speak to her myself - but very gently."

We were going off that morning to a little lake some dozen miles off to try for a jack or two. Franziska was coming with us. She was, indeed, already outside, superintending the placing in the trap of our rods and bags. When Charlie went out she said that everything was ready; and presently our peasant driver cracked his whip, and away we went.

Charlie was a little grave, and could only reply to Tita's fun with an effort. Franziska was mostly anxious about the fishing, and hoped that we might not go so far to find nothing.

We found few fish anyhow. The water was as still as

glass, and as clear; the pike that would have taken our spinning bits of metal must have been very dull-eyed pike indeed. Tita sat at the bow of the long punt reading, while our boatman steadily and slowly plied his single oar. Franziska was for a time eagerly engaged in watching the progress of our fishing, until even she got tired of the excitement of rolling in an immense length of cord, only to find that our spinning bait had hooked a bit of floating wood or weed. At length Charlie proposed that he should go ashore and look out for a picturesque site for our picnic, and he hinted that perhaps Miss Franziska might also like a short walk to relieve the monotony of the sailing. Miss Franziska said she would be very pleased to do that. We ran them in among the rushes, and put them ashore, and then once more started on our laborious career.

Tita laid down her book. She was a little anxious. Sometimes you could see Charlie and Franziska on the path by the side of the lake; at other times the thick trees by the water's side hid them.

The solitary oar dipped in the lake; the boat glided along the shores. Tita took up her book again. The space of time that passed may be inferred from the fact that, merely as an incident to it, we managed to catch a chub of four pounds. When the excitement over this event had passed, Tita said:

"We must go back to them. What do they mean by not coming on and telling us? It is most silly of them."

We went back by the same side of the lake, and we found both Franziska and her companion seated on the bank at the precise spot where we had left them. They said it was the best place for the picnic. They asked for the hamper in a businesslike way. They pretended they had searched the shores of the lake for miles.

And while Tita and Franziska are unpacking the things, and laying the white cloth smoothly on the grass, and pulling out the bottles for Charlie to cool in the lake, I observe that the younger of the two ladies rather endeavours to keep her left hand out of sight. It is a paltry piece of deception. Are we moles, and blinder than moles, that we should continually be made the dupes of these women? I say to her:

"Franziska, what is the matter with your left hand?"

"Leave Franziska's left hand alone," says Tita, severely.

"My dear," I reply, humbly, "I am afraid Franziska has hurt her left hand."

At this moment Charlie, having stuck the bottles among the reeds, comes back, and, hearing our talk, he says, in a loud and audacious way:

"Oh, do you mean the ring? It's a pretty little thing I had about me, and Franziska has been good enough to accept it. You can show it to them, Franziska.

Of course he had it about him. Young men always do carry a stock of ruby rings with them when they go fishing, to put in the noses of the fish. I have observed it frequently.

Franziska looks timidly at Tita, and then she raises her hand, that trembles a little. She is about to take the ring off to show it to us when Charlie interposes:

"You needn't take it off, Franziska."

And with that, somehow, the girl slips away from among us, and Tita is with her, and we don't get a glimpse of either of them until the solitude resounds with our cries for luncheon.

In due time Charlie returned to London, and to Surrey with us in very good spirits. He used to come down very often to see us; and one evening at dinner he disclosed the fact that he was going over to the Black Forest in the following week, although the November nights were chill just then.

"And how long do you remain?"

"A month," he says.

"Madam," I say to the small lady at the other end of the table," a month from now will bring us to the 4th of December. You have lost the bet you made last Christmas morning; when will it please you to resign your authority?"

"Oh, bother the bet," says this unscrupulous person.

"But what do you mean?" says Charlie.

"Why," I say to him, "she laid a wager last Christmas Day that you would not be married within a year. And now you say you mean to bring Franziska over on the 4th of December next. Isn't it so?"

"Oh, no!" he says; "we don't get married till

the spring."

You should have heard the burst of low, delightful laughter with which Queen Tita welcomed this announcement. She had won her wager.

www.ingramcontent.com/pod-product-compliance
Lightning Source LLC
Chambersburg PA
CBHW020548310726
48979CB00008B/1137/J

* 9 7 8 1 4 2 1 8 0 8 7 9 6 *